THE ARCHIP
OF ANOTHER LIFE

Andreï Makine

THE ARCHIPELAGO
OF ANOTHER LIFE

Translated from the French by
Geoffrey Strachan

MACLEHOSE PRESS
QUERCUS · LONDON

First published in the French language as *L'archipel d'une autre vie*
by Éditions du Seuil, Paris, in 2016
First published in Great Britain in 2019 by MacLehose Press
This paperback edition published in 2020 by

MacLehose Press
an imprint of Quercus Publishing Ltd
Carmelite House
50 Victoria Embankment
London EC4Y 0DZ

An Hachette UK company

A CIP catalogue record for this book is available from the British Library.

ISBN (MMP) 978 0 85705 794 5
ISBN (Ebook) 978 0 85705 792 1

10 9 8 7 6 5 4 3 2 1

Designed and typeset in Albertina by Libanus Press, Marlborough
Printed and bound in Great Britain by Clays Ltd, Elcograf S.p.A.

MIX
Paper from
responsible sources
FSC® C104740

Papers used by MacLehose Press are from well-managed forests
and other responsible sources.

TRANSLATOR'S NOTE

ANDREÏ MAKINE WAS BORN AND BROUGHT UP IN RUSSIA but *The Archipelago of Another Life*, like his other novels, was written in French. The book is set mainly in Russia. The author employs some Russian and Siberian words in the French text, which I have retained in this English translation. These include *izba* (a traditional wooden house built of logs), *taiga* (the swampy coniferous forest of northern latitudes that lies between the tundra and the steppes), *ukase* (a decree with the force of law), *taimen* (a kind of Siberian salmon trout), *stlanik* (a thicket of low horizontal cedar trees unique to the coastal fringes of Siberia), *gulag* (the system of corrective labour camps, of which the Kolyma complex was the most notorious), *apparatchik* (a member of the Soviet Communist Party administration or *apparat*), *kolkhoz* (a collective farm in the former Soviet Union), *kamus* (hide from reindeer legs) and *souloi* (a high wall of water created where opposing ocean currents meet).

References to the earth's prehistory in the text include Rodinia, the supercontinent assembled some 1.5 billion years ago; Mirovia, the hypothesised superocean that surrounded it; and Panthalassa, the ocean into which it developed.

I am indebted to many people, and the author in particular, for advice, assistance and encouragement given to me during the preparation of this translation. To all of them my thanks are due and, in addition to Andreï Makine himself, notably to June Elks, Paul Engles, Scott Grant, Willem Hackman, Russell Ingham, Robina Pelham Burn, Simon Strachan, Susan Strachan, John and Anne Weeks, Helen Williams and Jim and Sarah Woodhouse.

G.S.

For Anne Granval

For Lieutenant Schreiber

I

AT THAT MOMENT IN MY YOUTH THE VERB "TO LIVE" took on a new meaning for me. Now it could really only be used when speaking of those two who had made it to the distant seas around the Shantar Islands. For all other forms of activity here on earth the word "exist" would suffice.

I had just set out to walk inland, away from the shore, when a helicopter disrupted the misty drowsiness of the morning. The only flight of the week for the little village of Tugur, a remote spot on the Pacific coast. The passengers disembarked, laden with suitcases, shopping bags, rolls of carpet . . . There was momentary confusion between those who had just emerged and those gathered on the landing strip, waiting to board the aircraft. A woman was describing her visit to the cinema (an event!); a man was stuffing a folding bed into his sidecar; a newcomer, shivering in her light clothes, was seeking information from the locals . . .

I decided to wait until everyone had left before setting off again. And it was then that I noticed this other man among the arrivals.

Seated at the foot of a rock, he was checking his pack, which had a hunter's skis strapped to it. These were very short and broad, covered with *kamus*, the tough hide from the legs of reindeer. In these parts snow could catch the traveller unawares even in summer. The traveller . . . I sensed that this man would not be stopping in the village, nor would he be joining the flight. His goal lay elsewhere.

This notion formed a bond between us, like a shared secret. We could both see the same ash-grey outline of the mountains, the sunlight on the fragments of seashells and, beneath a mass of weed, slabs of ice that defied the July warmth . . . I felt very close to this stranger. But there was a stubborn mystery about him – his was an identity more complex than that of a simple trapper from the taiga.

The helicopter roared, throwing up a cloud of pine needles, took off and quickly became a tiny dot above the sea.

The man got up, and shouldered his burden, dancing a little on the spot to balance it better. Without noticing me watching him from a hollow in the dunes.

Stepping away from the strip of foreshore that is so convenient in these lands with no roads, he plunged into the forest, and instantly sought to make himself invisible. I followed in the wake of his passage – the snapping of a branch, a plant stem pressed down. He left few traces.

My arrival in Tugur, a week before, had seemed like a classic confirmation of the verdict the "sovietologists" of those days were given to pronouncing on Russia and her ageing communist regime, at a time which coincided with our own youth.

At the end of the school year our class was divided into two and an announcement was made: the first group would be trained as crane operators, the second as land surveyors . . . At the age of fourteen we manifested differing aptitudes and, despite the levelling down of orphanage life, both exceptionally gifted students and dunces could be found among us, beastly Stakhanovites as well as incorrigible idlers. An ukase from the Party smoothed over these differences. From central Siberia they shipped us off two and a half thousand miles eastwards to the Pacific shores of the Soviet empire, where both apprentice crane operators and novice land surveyors were required on a construction site.

"Totalitarian regimentation", the sovietologists would pontificate, "the dictatorial denial of human individuality". Yes, no doubt . . . Except that this was not something we were experiencing in theory, but in every fibre of our young souls, both carefree and full of sorrow, hungry for love and nursing disappointed hopes. Our departure blended into the dazzling skies and vibrant smells of the taiga, where the sap was just rising. In rebellion against all doctrines, we had only one desire: to succumb to the intoxication of this new spring, convinced it would be the best of our lives.

The starting point for our apprenticeship was Nikolayevsk, on the left bank of the river Amur, "just an hour from the Pacific", we were proudly informed. But we had no chance to see the ocean, we were stuck there on the shores of the estuary.

The only mental image I had of land surveying was of two men, one holding a calibrated pole, the other with his eye glued to an optical device mounted on a tripod. Our training period did little to enhance this basic notion. Making scant use of precision in their terminology, our masters would refer to their apparatus as "the doodah", "the whatsit" or, more emphatically, "all this sodding stuff". Their pedagogical laxness left us plenty of time to explore the port and inhale the sea breezes, mild indeed, compared with the harsh, dry, continental air of inland Siberia.

After work we often chanced to see our instructors in an open-air refreshment bar facing onto the docks. One evening we surprised them there with a member of the fair sex: glamour had been added to the staunch duo, whom we had thought to be inseparable, by the presence of a woman with luminous blond hair. And yet, she was visibly causing a rift between them, for the Big Guy and the Little Guy (as we called them) were now at daggers drawn. Two empty bottles lay on the ground beside the "whatsits" and the tripod . . . They were sparring by flaunting their professional skills: each boasting of his exploits in land surveying. From the way they were talking it sounded as if they had both of them completed topographical surveys all over Russia. A whole cavalcade of sites, each one more improbable than the last, paraded past: from a sports palace to a naval base; from an Olympic stadium to a rocket-launching site . . . Their guest sipped her wine with an enigmatic smile. And at last we were learning the correct terminology! In their male competitiveness, our instructors were now holding forth about goniometers, tachometers and theodolites...

It was hard for a woman to choose between them: the Big Guy was a fine figure of a man, but the Little Guy sported a leather jacket, something that in those days assured a Russian of real social status.

"My next job's going to be with the Japanese," the Big Guy asserted, "doing a survey for a wharf..."

The shameless mendaciousness of this purported assignment infuriated the Little Guy.

"You? With the Japanese? But you don't know one end of a graphometer from the other!"

This was a monstrous insult. The Big Guy rose to his feet, grabbed his rival and hit him. The latter avoided falling over but slipped on a bottle and ended up performing a rather long and unintentionally obscene jerk dance. The customers roared with laughter. The fair-haired charmer giggled. The Little Guy flushed crimson and the situation turned ugly. He seized the tripod that was equipped with steel spikes, uttered a hoarse yell and shoved it into the Big Guy's chest. The crunch of broken ribs was followed by an "Ooh!" from the audience, then silence. The Big Guy thrust aside the weapon that had now fallen at his feet, unbuttoned his padded tunic with a grave face, and plunged his hand inside. We stood up to get a better view of the mangled flesh and bone he was about to draw forth from within . . . His hand reappeared: it was holding a notebook whose imitation leather cover was marked with three deep indentations. The record book in which he used to note our results . . . The spectators felt vaguely disappointed. Then the Big Guy picked up the tripod, took off the legs and suddenly, in a neat movement, trapped his adversary's neck in the angle between them. The Little Guy collapsed, trying to remove this vice, struggled, weakened. With his wine-stained tongue protruding, he was at his last gasp. Knocking over their chairs, the men leaped up, the women wailed. And the lady of discord beat a retreat, leaving us, as she departed, with a cloud of sugary perfume and a dazzling flash of thigh through the slit in her velvet skirt . . . Already the dockers' heavy mitts were prising open the garrotte. Beside these men, with their thick, knotty muscles and tattoos, the Big Guy looked like some refined intellectual.

We spent that evening re-enacting the brawl. Laughter, fisticuffs, lewd remarks about the blonde seductress . . . But what our antics really betrayed was a certain unease. There was no risk of our being traumatised by that pedagogical apocalypse at the dockside bar – we were used to witnessing more brutal confrontations than that. But there was nevertheless a hidden agenda lurking behind the facade of that farcical duel.

That night the boy next to me in the dormitory (we were lodged in a former fishing net factory), a sickly lad, not very popular with the others, began sobbing, his face buried in his pillow. His tears, which contravened our strict codes of honour, might have provoked our scorn. But nobody moved a muscle. We knew his father had died in a camp, not so far from the site of our training session. Unlike the rest of us, who invented heroic career paths for our dead parents, this boy used to tell the truth: since the permafrost made it impossible to bury prisoners who died during the winter, they would be stockpiled like yule logs until the mild weather returned. Thus it was that his father had had to wait until the spring to be buried. "He lingered on there among the living," our comrade must have mused as a child ... "Anyone could have gone over to him and woken him up." His tears that night had been set off by that ludicrous dust-up between our two masters – a life that was stupid and theatrical, one of insatiable desires, one that paid little heed to a prisoner asleep in his shroud of ice ...

Such is the way the world works! In fighting over a woman, men would play all their aces: an athletic physique, professional status, banknotes with Lenin's face on them, or, as the occasion demanded, that tripod crushing the Adam's apple of a rival.

I had just grasped the crude machinery of existence. Our teachers had revealed it to us at their own humble level, that of two poor sods of land surveyors who would stop at nothing to sleep with a peroxide blonde. And the rest of mankind? Naturally, the same game of conquerors and conquered. The Big Guy and the Little Guy had only their tripod as a weapon. Others had guns, wealth, power – and prison camps – at their disposal ...

So everything in life revolved around a beautiful woman's thigh – the universal drama of rivalry, seduction, mute hatred and garrulous mendacity. Along with those pleasant moments of relaxation in a café bar on the banks of the Amur ... And a child weeping for his father, unable to wake him from his ice-bound lethargy.

Such were the real lessons of my land surveyor's apprenticeship.

The next day I lost all desire for conquest. The most aggressive members of our group won the privilege of continuing their training at Nikolayevsk, others were dispersed to nearby locations. I found I was the only one to be despatched to Tugur, the least sought-after destination on the list.

Our educators no longer showed any signs of mutual hostility. No doubt they had arrived at an honourable peace over their last bottle ... The Big Guy was calling out our names from his pierced notebook and, oblivious of the comic aspect of the situation, advising us to grease the spikes of the tripod liberally against rust.

TUGUR, TWO HOURS' FLIGHT FROM THERE BY HELICOPTER, gave me visions of an endless, empty coastline opening out onto an awe-inspiring prospect, the rolling expanse of the Pacific. At our age we all had dreams of Mirovia, the legendary superocean, and the prehistoric waters of Panthalassa.

Since nobody came to meet me when I got there, I rushed down to the shore. The day was dawning and, unable to believe my eyes, I went galloping through the dunes, in search of the hoped-for vastness, a giddy encounter with the ocean itself . . .

In reality Tugur was located at the head of an inlet squeezed between precipitous slopes which led, as I would later discover, into modest coastal waters. A small archipelago formed a barrier between these and the Sea of Okhotsk, which itself then opened out into the Pacific Ocean.

What lay before me was very beautiful: sandy beaches, the mouths of several streams, mirror-like pools . . . But no sign of Mirovia on the horizon!

That village of maybe a hundred inhabitants had no real need of a trainee. The team of land surveyors I was supposed to be attached to had been retained in Nikolayevsk, the town

I had just left . . . They housed me in a shack partly occupied by an edge tool maker's workshop, showed me a canteen used by fishermen and forgot about me.

In my first exploration I set off towards a headland where I reckoned I would finally be able to admire the ocean, the real ocean. But when I reached it all I could see was the next headland – and the sea, still held captive by a series of bays, contained within sandbanks . . . Bounded waters hiding the boundless ocean from view.

After passing a week there, following my arrival, I felt I wanted to get away from these maritime optical illusions and revisit the taiga, a world I had always felt at home in since my childhood. In my bag I took with me some dried fish, one of those old-style tinder boxes, where the wick has nothing to fear from the wind, and a hatchet, borrowed from the edge tool maker. He had also lent me an old padded jacket stained with grease.

Just as I was turning my back on the shore the noise of a helicopter punctured the silence. A minute later I saw the passengers busying themselves amid the luggage. And close to a rock, that traveller, waiting until he could slip away without being seen.

Nothing distinguished him from the inhabitants of Tugur, apart, perhaps, from his leather hood. His tanned face was that of a nomad, but here, between sea and forest, nobody was a stay-at-home.

However, he seemed aloof from the regular workings of

mankind, as I had come to understand them, thanks to that brawl between our masters: the interplay of desires, competing vanities, the whole charade of striking poses – everything that people believe to be life itself. This aloofness of his suggested time spent in unusual concentration and, with it, the gradual erosion of the names given to beings and objects . . .

Such thriftiness with words made me uneasy. I was impatient to identify this man. A poacher? Or one of those covert prospectors for gold sometimes encountered on the pathways through the taiga? Made feral by their solitary existence, and sensing danger at the least trace of any human presence, they were forever in pursuit of their cherished fantasy: to amass a stash of nuggets, to abandon this icy hell, to settle on the shores of the Black Sea, and to make love to all those tanned women, the succulent succubi who have haunted their dreams for so many years . . .

The helicopter sliced through the mist, took off, disappeared. The new arrivals, burdened with luggage, made their way towards the izbas of Tugur. One snatch of their talk reached me: a young woman, the newcomer, a native of Odessa, was telling them about her journey. The man sitting beside the rock must have been thinking, as I was: Odessa, the Black Sea . . . That's six thousand miles from here . . .

He stood up, shouldered his kit and set off walking. And, as I followed his trail, I felt he was not a total stranger to me.

"Walking" in the taiga is only a manner of speaking. In reality you have to pass through it with the suppleness of a swimmer.

Anyone who tries to thrust, smash and force a path through it quickly exhausts himself, reveals his presence and ends up loathing all those waves of tree branches, heather and brush-wood as they break over him.

The man with the hood knew this. He bent double to pass through the thickets of young spruces in places where another person might have set about pushing their entangled branches aside and taken three times as long . . . Elsewhere, I saw him stepping along with rolling strides (it reminded me of a land surveyor's cross staff), the only way to navigate a *stlanik*, one of the stretches of "creeping woodland" which are, in fact, dwarf pine trees, an inextricable tangle, a snare at every step. A danger-ous spot – bears relish the pine kernels from these midget trees.

Faced with a small river, he judged the water level at a glance, avoided the milky part of the stream (a clay bottom, therefore slippery) and made a detour towards a ford, where there were pebbles . . .

I was delighted to notice these details – my own experience, far inland, was still valid in these forests of eastern Siberia. Some unaccustomed plants, some unfamiliar profiles of hills and valleys, but the same traces of animals, the same signs indicating varying types of soil. The vocabulary of this forest was familiar, although there were some minor differences, thanks to the proximity of the coast. One such difference gave me a fright: a giant spider, with legs as long as my arm, protruding from the moss! Going up to it, I unearthed the remains of a huge crab from the Sea of Okhotsk that had been a meal for some kind of fish hawk.

Weariness was gradually brought on by the alternation of the lines of sky and greenery unfolding before me – before us, for he and I kept pace with one another – and I could sense the choices the wanderer was making in places where the way led uphill, as well as his pleasure at shedding his load, wading into a stream and splashing his face and neck, now covered with pollen from the pine trees.

I became aware of this link between our two solitudes, his and mine, at the moment when he made a halt. He did not light a fire, but ate some dried fish, like me, and drank water from the stream.

I felt bad about spying on him like this, violating a private moment in his life. Should I go up to him? Ask his forgiveness for stalking him? My youthful spirit of adventure bridled at this: no, I was going to track him down, discover his stash, get my hands on his gold! And treat myself to . . . To what, exactly? I thought about our training instructors, the Big Guy and the Little Guy: they epitomised the idea of certain measures of success. A cheap Toyota that you could pick up in a dock-side town for the price of several years' hard work, a bottle of port wine from Azerbaijan to share with a blonde in a velvet skirt . . .

The stranger concluded his meal. Motionless, he gazed at the stream rippling with long cascades of sunlight . . . In truth, this was all I wanted: to be just where he was, dwelling in this silence, wordlessly understanding what it meant for me to be lingering here at this time.

The man rose to his feet, picked up his pack and paused, as

23

if seeking to emphasise what I had just grasped: the utter joy of living in this moment.

Halfway through the afternoon a fine drizzle brought darkness to the underwood. As I skirted a marshy dell I admitted to myself that, without my "guide", I should have had difficulty in finding a way through.

After emerging from the peat bog, I lost sight of him. No crackle of a twig, no swaying branch to signal his passing. I had to go back the way I had come in order to pick up his trail, very deep footprints, on account of his load.

Losing my way like this made me nervous. Especially since we were crossing a stlanik of dwarf pine trees. A childhood memory: a quiet foraging trip in woodland like this and all of a sudden the sight of a brown hillock rearing up . . . A female bear! The lashing of branches, our vision fragmented by fear, the great leaps we performed as we fled – by instinct we were imitating roe deer, who know how to extricate themselves from the snare of the stlanik. Our dog comes running up (where was your sense of smell, idiot?), his barking stops the bear in her tracks, she is keener on protecting her cubs than devouring us fugitives.

The man's hood came into view again, too close now, and looked as if it was no longer moving forwards. I stopped, to keep my distance. After all, he might be relieving himself.

Suddenly the air seemed to grow dense with menace. Some creature was eyeing me! From behind these larches? Or over there in those thickets? I already had my back against the trunk of a tree, ready to strike with my hatchet. A bear would have growled, made a noise ... Wolves? They generally attack in open terrain. And besides, in July they are too well fed. These rapid calculations did not stop me peering hard at every possible hiding place, pricking up my ears for the faintest rustling sounds. No, nothing suspicious. And yet I knew I was being observed.

The air cleared, my feeling of being in danger faded. In the distance the hooded man was moving up a slope. In an admission of weakness, the thought occurred to me that, had I been attacked, he would surely have come to my rescue.

As the evening approached, the sky lit up, spilling a golden translucence over the taiga that had previously been darkened by drizzle. I reflected that the stranger must soon reach his shelter or would be setting up a camp ...

He climbed up onto a little hill surmounted by a mass of rock, stopped there and gazed into the distance at what was invisible to me from down below. On his face I believed I could discern a smile. The low sun gave his silhouette an unreal intensity. He was alone in the universe ...

I was preparing to follow him down the slope on the far side of the hill, but he retraced his footsteps back into the forest, passing close by, but without noticing me. He must still have been dazzled by the radiance that held sway on the hilltop.

Going down to the stream we had been following for hours, he decided to set up camp. To make sure of this, I waited for him to light a fire. The flames leaped up and I became invisible – now all he would see would be their dancing glow in the darkness.

I moved away, following a loop in the stream, picked up driftwood dried by the sun, and lit two fires: one of them would burn throughout the night, the other would warm the ground. Its embers, well trodden down and covered in sand and branches, would retain their heat for a long time . . . I lay down upon this warm couch and quickly fell asleep.

Soon I had to add more wood to my fire. Then sleep overcame me again, for as long as the flames lasted.

Some time later I woke up and became aware that my fire was still burning brightly. Too brightly! Propping myself up on one elbow I consulted my watch: past midnight. So, since the last time I woke, I had slept for over an hour. And the flames had not died down. Impossible! I tried to think . . .

Suddenly, behind me, I caught sight of another source of light.

I spun round and what I saw froze me. A dozen yards away from my encampment a more discreet fire was glowing but not blazing. A man seated on a fallen tree trunk that was half buried in sand had his back to me. His head, covered by a hood, was bowed over the embers. He did not stir. Asleep?

A minute dragged by as I held my breath. I knew what would be my escape route – leap over to the bank of the stream, run the length of that copse of elders and then, in three final strides, dive deep into the darkness of the *taiga*.

Grasping my bag, I tensed my body like a bow, thrust against the ground and jumped up . . .

And four steps later I fell over, my right foot brought to a halt. The flames gave enough light for me to see a running noose around my ankle. The other end of the cord was attached to the trunk of the tree on which the stranger sat.

Slowly, with a sigh halfway between yawning and irritation, the man got up, came over to my fire and extracted a hefty brand from it.

He stood upright over me and at his belt I saw a long dagger in a leather sheath. Without a word, he brought the torch close to my face. Thinking he was about to thrust it into my eyes, I closed my eyelids tight shut. He gave a cough, as if saying to himself, "It's just as I thought."

Returning to his own fire, he threw the brand into it, sat down and turned his back on me. I did not dare get up, too anxious about what might happen next. Would he let me go and run the risk of being denounced? But what did he have to hide? His gold? An escape? A murder? The tales of our youth were peopled by such outlaws, who did not hesitate to rid themselves of inquisitive strangers, when caught unawares on their secret paths . . . I bent my leg and began wrestling with the noose.

The man gave a brief whistle, grasped the cord and tugged on it. His voice was calm.

"Take that off and come over here."

I hastened to obey him, fiddled nervously with the hemp cord, freed myself and went over to him. With a nod of his head he indicated a bundle of wood on the other side of his fire.

"Sit down . . . So, what's your story?"

BY THE END OF FIVE MINUTES, I RECKONED I HAD TOLD HIM everything: our exodus from the orphanage, the work experience programme, the dust-up between the land surveyors, Tugur . . . I even confessed my intention of stealing his gold.

He growled, "A fine plan indeed, young man. But fair's fair. We don't cut off a penitent's head."

He set down a tin teapot covered in soot into the glowing embers, and added: "Now this is real gold. Drink a cup of this and you'll be good for thirty miles . . . And you ought to know that those crafty fellows who do their sifting on the quiet always protect their precious nuggets very well. They put a bear trap in front of their stash. You make a grab for the bag and quick as a flash, your leg's shackled. Then all you have to do is wait for some animal to come and devour you."

He broke off now, out of respect for the tea ceremony, even though what we were drinking was an infusion of wild rose and pine shoots. I was quietly studying him: plain, open features, a broad scar on his neck and several marks on one cheek, doubtless the traces of frostbite long ago. At my age I judged him to be "old", that is to say in his forties. The fact that he was clearly at home in the taiga did not fully explain his odd manner. Other traits revealed it better: facial expressions too subtle for the range of emotions a man of his stamp needed to convey, a rough way of speaking muted by a dreamy, melancholic intonation . . .

I was thinking about this as I watched him going to fetch some water. His momentary absence left a disturbing vacuum. I could easily have run away, yes. But staying with him was changing the meaning of what I knew of life. He came back, placed his teapot among the hot embers. His gaze settled upon me as if he did not recognise me. It seemed as if my case was decided: the next day he would continue on his way, and I, like a child judged to be at fault but pardoned, would return to Tugur . . . Sensing my mood of vexation, he adopted tones of camaraderie.

"So how goes it with school? You told me you were at a 'special establishment'. What does this speciality consist of? Stalking strangers in the middle of the taiga, is that it?"

Proud to resume our conversation, man to man, I clarified that phrase of mine: all the pupils in our orphanage had parents who had died in the camps. We had been hived off there so that we did not contaminate ordinary schools, where we would have divulged what happens to prisoners. Cooped up together, we did not have much of a tale to tell. Our life histories were similar and therefore banal. Parents who had died in inglorious circumstances, crushed beneath tree trunks, unloaded off tractors, beaten to death by fellow prisoners, killed by a guard or dead from exhaustion and disease . . .

"Would you like more tea?"

His voice was oddly insistent. Was he seeking to steer me away from a painful topic? Sensing that he was uneasy, I cut short my tale.

"It's a boarding school like any other, except, you see, that we're all children of ..."

"Jailbirds ..." he cut in abruptly.

"Of prisoners," I snapped back, emphatically.

It was one of the inviolable rules in our world: we could freely heap insults upon one another but nobody must offend against the memory of our parents.

"Yes, prisoners, is what I meant to say ... Right, we're going to eat some taimen now. Mere salmon is small fry beside it ..."

His gestures became exaggeratedly relaxed. I had never seen an adult so embarrassed. We ate long delicate strips that smelled of smoke and juniper berries.

"The king of fish!"

This exclamation was at odds with the pained way he was looking at me. I thought I must have upset him with all that talk of prison camps. To change the subject, I asked him about something that intrigued me. "So tell me, at what stage did you notice I was following you?"

He timed his riposte like an old campaigner.

"At what stage? Oh, from the start. There's a trick: you go into the forest, you take a few steps, then you slip behind a fir tree and turn round, to see if there's anyone on your tail. Later on there'll be too much undergrowth for you to be able to tell ..."

This conversation of ours was skating over something that

was becoming increasingly apparent to me: it was merely habit that made my life in that "specialised orphanage" seem banal. In order to cheat our pain we had all woven a veil of legends that glorified our dead parents. The man with the hood had just torn it aside.

He must have been aware of this, for his anxiety went well beyond mere pity for "the children of jailbirds". I sensed that, in some mysterious way, this wanderer had something in common with us all . . .

My next question was a routine one.

"This afternoon there was some creature watching me. What could it have been? Was it a wolf that had strayed from its pack . . . ?"

He responded in a somewhat uncertain imitation of a huntsman's bravado. "Aha, no, that was me, coming to see if my pursuer threatened serious mischief. That great jacket of yours made you appear older . . ."

"But I could see your hood high up on a hill."

"My hood comes off. I hung it on a branch and went down to take a look at you. The wolf with no pack was me . . ."

We both smiled, less at the phrase than from a new shared understanding. The man's voice resumed its calm timbre.

"Tell me, how old were you when your parents . . . passed away?"

I managed to choke back the pain inherent in the words I found.

"They told me my father had been arrested two months before I was born. As for my mother, she had me in the camp

. . . There was a nursery section for newborn babies. And then . . . two years later, she died."

I guessed that he was going to ask me the painful question I have always managed to avoid. In my mind I was searching for a way to sidestep it. Should I ask him the name of the river that was murmuring there in the darkness? Or enquire where his walk was leading him?

He articulated his words in a measured way.

"And so . . . your mother, did you never know her?"

"I did, I think I saw her . . . Once."

I was unable to stir now, my gaze fixed on the teapot there among the embers, which was giving off a wisp of steam. I was blinded by a vision that had been studiously suppressed: a very young child is lying in his bed, a woman comes over to him and kisses him and, without his being able to see her clearly in the darkness, he is overwhelmed by her tenderness. The woman leaves and, before the door closes on her, he glimpses her face streaked with tears and her lips murmuring words whose melody he rediscovers in his sleep . . .

A rigid struggle against a sob was tearing my chest. If the man had spoken to me then, I should not have been able to contain an explosion of distress. But he stood up, seized the teapot and strode off into the darkness.

When he returned, a quarter of an hour later, the fire was almost out. I had recovered my composure and felt strangely aged. That moment from my childhood seemed to hold within it all the love and all the pain that I would come to know in the course of a whole lifetime.

The man replenished the teapot with his herbal mixture, and sat down facing me on the tree trunk with the cord attached to it, the one that had snared me. He unfastened it, rolled it up, stowed it in his bag . . . And began speaking very softly, as he poked the embers.

"It was in Stalin's time, before you were born. One day I . . . Well, this fellow whose name was Pavel . . . Pavel Gartsev . . . thought he was going to be able to live a life just the way other people did . . ."

Hesitantly to begin with, as if he had first had to reassume the identity of a certain Pavel Gartsev, he continued his story, conjuring up an "I" of long ago, more believable to others than to himself.

"In those years, 1949, 1950, the planet could well have vanished . . . The Korean War. The Americans were ready to do another Hiroshima, by bombing Maoist China, our ally. But the message got through in time: Russia had just acquired her own bomb. The tests had exceeded all expectations, burning to a cinder vast areas of desert, concrete structures, livestock that had been stationed there to enhance the value of the test, and even, so it was said, a number of prisoners under sentence of death. All that was left was a mirror of vitrified sand. Reconnaissance planes saw themselves reflected in it, as in a lake. And, by the way, so monstrous was the radiation level that the pilots of those aircraft died within two days. At that time I knew nothing about these tests. And yet it was an early blueprint for World War Three that was about to change my life . . ."

He fell silent, frowned, tossed his head, as if to clear himself a path through the dense thickets of the years. His voice adopted tones of an ironic melancholy that I was already familiar with.

"The fact is that one evening I came back home at a bad moment . . . But wait, let me tell you the story from the beginning."

II

"YES, I CAME HOME AT A BAD MOMENT THAT EVENING..."
The man paused, searching for the words that might best
convey this story of his life to the adolescent that I was...

It was June 1952, I was twenty-seven and about to get married
to a girl of just eighteen, Sveta... I was convinced that finally
happiness would be within my grasp, an illusion one clings
to after a long period of darkness... The death of my parents,
twenty years earlier, had had nothing to do with Stalin's purges.
My father was in charge of the construction of a hydroelectric
station with a dam that was going to flood dozens of villages.
One of the locals managed to get onto the construction site
and set off an explosion of the stock of dynamite. The dam
collapsed and the office where my parents were working was
swept away...

My uncle took me to the site. Their drowning seemed beyond
my comprehension, my mother and father engulfed in a tide
of mud, and hurled into a black, yawning void. It was a vision
that took my breath away to the point of asphyxia.

Amid the cement debris I found a rag doll, the toy I had often seen in the hands of little Sima, the daughter of one of the site workers. That had been the first thrill of a childish love affair for me ... Now the sight of this scrap of fabric gave me a sense of the extreme vulnerability of my own body. That rag doll became embedded within me – like a kind of guardian angel that, from now on, would counsel caution, compromise, resignation.

At first the sympathetic looks other people gave me endowed me with a doleful but rewarding identity: me, Pavel Gartsev, victim of the enemies of socialism, practically a hero, a symbol.

Then one night I overheard a conversation between my uncle and aunt, with whom I was now living: the "enemy of socialism" who had dynamited the dam was in reality a deceived husband. My father had been having an affair with this technician's wife. The man had taken his revenge, underestimating the force of the explosion. He had merely intended to cause damage, so that my father should be accused of negligence and transferred ...

This revelation left in tatters the persona of a victim I had concocted for myself. Life was much more devious than that. It donned grimacing masks, took on a new tone, a revolutionary drama was transformed into a bedroom farce. Was I the child of dedicated communists laid low in a terrorist's coup? Or the son of a philanderer, who had received a harsh comeuppance?

In this confused world one constant prevailed: hatred. It could derive either from desire or from fear, or else from ideas that appeared to be noble, but, curiously enough, were the most lethal of all.

In 1937, on the day of the twentieth anniversary of the Revolution, construction work was resumed on the site. Shortly afterwards the new director of works would be arrested for "acts of anti-Soviet sabotage". I was already old enough to work it out: if a jealous husband had not killed my parents, they would now have been sent to a prison camp, along with all those thousands of managers accused of waste, sabotage and spying . . . In which case, as the offspring of these traitors to the country, I should have been sent to rot in a re-education camp.

The "rag doll" quaked within me: the wanton cruelty of these charades bore little resemblance to what they taught us in school and what I would later be learning at university.

Given my age group, I was not called up until 1943 when my posting was to serve in the editorial unit of a military newspaper. This was not a cushy number – war correspondents were embedded with fighting men. Typhus, war wounds, nights spent under snow, I had my fill of all of these and was even left with a souvenir, this mark made by a flame-thrower: a patch of burned skin on my neck. A blemish that looked like a spider gorged with blood.

There was also another after-effect, an invisible one, a scar on my memory: a town on the Baltic, an infantry unit I was advancing with as a reporter, houses gutted by bombs and, in one narrow alleyway, the bodies of a dozen women, trampled under foot by the soldiers as they ran, because, as we were coming under fire, there was no time for us to stop and lift them aside . . . Of all the carnage I witnessed, the fact of having trampled on a woman's face would haunt me with the most pitiless persistence . . .

When the war ended I went back to Leningrad and, after my degree studies, I began working towards a thesis on the subject of "the Marxist–Leninist concept of the legitimacy of revolutionary violence . . ." In embarking on this research I was pursuing a highly subjective interest: I wanted to understand what lay behind the simultaneously brutal and frivolous games of History. In short, the lives and deaths of my parents.

When I met Sveta, it felt like a return to the marvellous routines of peacetime life. Born in a small town over a hundred miles from Leningrad, she worked in a library and in the evenings was studying to become an accountant.

I had already had several relationships – the deaths of millions of soldiers made every man a rare commodity for lonely women. Ashamed of taking advantage of this dubious privilege, I found excuses: after all, I might well not have survived the slaughter myself, the "spider", that scar on my neck, offered blunt proof of that.

Sveta banished this brooding. She loved me as I was, while I, for my part, surprised myself by, for the first time, finding endearing even acts of clumsiness or forgetfulness in a woman. Yes, like leaving a pan on the stove or losing a key . . . With her air of dancing on clouds, how on earth could she ever learn accountancy?

The love I felt for her was made all the more fervent by this.

I planned to create a heaven apart for us. That was it, clouds for us both to dance on.

I believed in all of this so utterly that the notion of expounding my thesis to her did not strike me as incongruous. As she listened to me holding forth about Oliver Cromwell or the wars of the Vendée, she would frown, and that expression of a little girl concentrating hard made me long to cover the lines on her knitted brow with kisses. I would break off from my exposition, and draw her to me, encountering a body that was a little gauche, but felt as if it was on a faster learning curve than her mind, when grappling with the concept of "the dictatorship of the proletariat".

Sveta seemed not to notice my wound, that "spider" close to my carotid artery. And the love between us banished all memories of that narrow alleyway strewn with the corpses of women.

One day, however, this new life, that was so precious to me, was turned inside out, in a revelation that set me on quite a different path ...

In the communal apartment where six families lived and where we occupied a room, the bathroom was much in demand. That morning I was shaving, trying not to scrape the burn on my neck: a routine which involved twisting my face this way and that, during which I left the door ajar so that other people should not cause me to botch this delicate operation by knocking loudly. No-one came and disturbed me, but suddenly, reflected in the depths of that old mirror, I glimpsed a look. I had never been stared at with such hostility! I turned round, convinced I was going to catch sight of an elderly female neighbour who was the bane of our lives scowling at me. But what was vanishing down the corridor was a blue nightdress worn by Sveta...

I wiped the mirror, as if to rid it of that vision, stared hard at myself – yes, there was indeed a "spider" on my neck, more visible after shaving, and one such as a woman might have sought to avoid brushing with her lips. A woman, that is, who had no affection for me ... A slight nick had caused a bead of blood to appear on the puffy edge of the scar.

But nothing changed between us. Sveta gave herself to me with the same adolescent gaucheness, addressing me in a mischievous whisper as "my pet". Without too much effort I succeeded in turning a blind eye.

A week after this look intercepted in the mirror, I received a notice from the city's military committee: all reservists were to report for two days of briefing prior to mobilisation. I was not displeased to be putting on my uniform and appearing before Sveta in my warrior's guise. Subconsciously, I hoped this would make my scarred neck more acceptable – for a soldier such war wounds were natural.

At the garrison, close to Leningrad, a colonel spoke to us about the fighting in Korea, the threat to the peace presented by American imperialism and the likelihood of anything from five to ten Hiroshimas occurring – but this time in cities in our own eastern territories...

Anxious to get back to Sveta as quickly as possible, I obtained permission to go home without waiting for the lorries that were due to take us all back that evening.

As I made my way into the courtyard to our block of flats, via Leningrad's noted network of winding alleys, night was falling. At that moment headlights began raking the space between the buildings and made me retreat towards the gateway. "Who's that idiot charging into the middle of the yard like this?" A car drew up, and by the light of a lamp above the front steps, I recognised Vlas Yulin, a university colleague who had already several times invited me round to his place, on the past few occasions with Sveta. Three years younger than me, he was making rapid progress in his career, thanks to his parents, high-ups in the Party. That car, the German generals' Horch 901, was a "trophy" his father had brought back from Berlin . . .

Sveta emerged from it and this made me think it must be some trick they had prepared for me. Then she kissed Yulin and their bodies locked together in a pose they were visibly familiar with. "Let me stay," he hissed in an excited whisper. She sniggered. "No chance. You know my roasted crab'll be back any minute now. Tomorrow I'll have found out how much time he's going to spend playing his war games. Then we can pass a few days together, my pet . . ." She broke away from him, climbed up the three steps and disappeared into the entrance hall.

To interrupt this scene I should have had to skirt round the car and thus lose the advantage of surprise. And besides, Sveta's words had left me paralysed. There was her "my pet", which was how she had also addressed Yulin. And that "roasted crab", no doubt their private nickname for me . . . This turnaround in the sense of all we had lived through left me dumbfounded.

The fact that it was impossible for me to make a dramatic intervention calmed me down, and prevented any violent or ridiculous behaviour on my part. Borne in on the wind were the scent of dust moistened by rain and the coolness of foliage. Stunned, I felt as if I could have melted into the night air, its scents, its silence . . . But I had to go home, step back into the role I was playing in life.

Sveta had already gone to bed and that made my performance easier. I ate, washed, lay down beside her. Half asleep she snuggled up to me . . . I could not see her face, but I sensed a certain hesitation: at that moment she did not know who she was. A young fiancée naively responding to love? Or a body that had little to learn about the mechanics of desire? I embraced her gently, hoping to rediscover the woman I loved . . . She let herself be possessed, without my being able to tell if she was feigning youthful inexperience or simply feeling sleepy. Suddenly, at the climax of pleasure, she whispered with a strident hiss: "Yes, my pet, yes!" and her movements took on the practised skill of one with a full knowledge of the techniques of carnality . . .

I thrust her away and sat there on the bed, preparing to make her admit the truth. But she had fallen asleep again, emitting wheezing snores, like an elderly woman worn out by life and had doubtless not even noticed my brutality.

That night, more grievously than ever, that wartime memory came back to me: a narrow alleyway littered with the corpses of women. They were patients from a psychiatric hospital, the townspeople had told us, mentally ill women, slaughtered by the Germans on the eve of our offensive.

I set off early in the morning, promising myself that I would throw light on everything that evening, after my return. "She'll come back with that shit, Yulin. I'll put them on the spot and then . . ." I found it hard to imagine how all this could end. A fight? A break with her? A tearful confession? All equally ludicrous and empty alternatives.

The second day at the garrison ended with an announcement that gave rise to jubilation on the part of most of the reservists, now free to go, and dejection among the rest whom the army was calling up for an indefinite period. "Depending on the political situation!" the colonel declared.

I was one of this minority who must now prepare for departure. Our kitbags were already packed. The next day we were to report to the railway station at 5.00 a.m.

I got home before Sveta's return, certain that Yulin would be coming back with her, as on the previous evening. I settled down on a bench beside a bush in a corner of the courtyard, an ideal spot for taking them by surprise.

I hardly had to wait at all. Sveta's voice rang out in the darkness – Yulin must have parked in the street. I stood up, my mind seething with reproaches. But very quickly I had to beat a retreat: she was coming on foot, followed by a woman!

The room I rented was on the ground floor. I saw the light go on, then the window was thrown open. It was very hot that

45

evening. My curiosity piqued almost more than on the previous night, I hugged the wall, stopping beneath the window that opened onto this room of mine, now lit up, both familiar and unrecognisable.

The two women were eating a modest supper, typical of the fare to be found in cities barely emerged from the war. I could hear brief remarks. As old acquaintances, they were compressing what they had to say to one another into allusions and sighs.

The gist of their conversation was totally devastating! The name of my "fiancée" was not Sveta but Zina, or at least that is what her friend was calling her. This Sveta-Zina was not eighteen but twenty-four. Like all the inhabitants of the rural zones under Stalin, she had no passport and was therefore living in Leningrad illegally. Her home town was not 120 miles away, amid beautiful forests, but less than twenty and it was a village destroyed by the war. The only people who lived there were widows and a handful of young "fiancées", ready to do anything to escape this little sliver of hell, without electricity, roads or shops. Yes, they were even ready to make love to a "roasted crab" . . .

Despite my bewilderment, I could understand the logic of Sveta's young life. After all, what the women I came across at the university were hoping for was precisely what she dreamed of: a husband, a family, a decent home. And her preference for someone like Yulin had nothing to do with my "roasted" neck, it was due to the more enviable station in life she calculated she could achieve, thanks to him. Sveta, the accountant.

I left the courtyard, my face set in a grimace of now pointless disgust, and decided to go to the station and spend the few remaining hours before my departure there. To leave without seeing Sveta again seemed to me the least painful course, but also the most appropriate: what could I say to this young woman whom, in truth, I had never met? A fictitious love affair cobbled together thanks to my foolish fondness . . . A piece of play-acting.

At the station rage and bitterness did not leave me at once. I pictured Sveta-Zina lavishing on Yulin caresses that I had been denied . . . In reality it was not about her anymore but the character invented by every man who has been deceived: a mistress, both hated and desired, all the more because she now belongs to another.

This rancour gave way to a realisation that suddenly dazzled me: "But what she's done is . . . She's set me free!" I imagined the sickening accumulation of lies that would have been my life with this woman, compelled to tolerate me and, inevitably, to suffer! And to put up with that "spider" on my neck.

In the train my fellow reservists smoked or drank tea laced with vodka. We were not raw recruits, but men who, for the most part, had been in the war. The officers did not impose too strict a discipline on us. Following a stop in Moscow, the train headed eastwards, having already been in transit for four days.

The subjects of conversation varied little: peevish wives, real millstones round our necks, who made life a misery, and, at the opposite extreme, lovers for one night who gave the world back its real savour. There was also talk of military exploits, based on the numbers of enemy killed. And talk of the relative advantages of different trades and the earnings they brought in. And, for some jammy bastards, that of having a car. Favourite football teams also figured. Values like these aroused no doubts in anyone.

Yes, Sveta had set me free from that life! I remembered my amorous plans, my jealousy. Henceforth silence reigned in that theatre of shadows, swept clean of all those lies.

After a further eight days we reached Amgun, a town located on a river of the same name. It then took us another day by road, in lorries, to reach the location where the simulation of the Third World War was to take place.

THIS TRAINING AREA, IN THE FAR EASTERN TAIGA, WAS designed to test our resistance in the event of an atomic conflict. The decision to send us to the other end of the country had already served as a means of checking if our army was capable of moving a large number of men closer to Japan and the American bases there. Early in the summer of 1952, a confrontation was becoming more and more likely.

There was nothing special about the manoeuvres we took part in: shooting, orientation on the terrain, parachute jumps. However, the distinctive element of nuclear warfare added a novel feature.

Over a distance of some twenty miles we made our way through the forest, consulting maps, wading deep into swamps . . . An exhausting task, given that we were rigged out in anti-atomic carapaces, gloves, masks and boots and a type of special suit that was as heavy as steel armour. To make the hypothetical radiation appear more spectacular, smoke grenades gave off a yellowish substance that hung in the air, also simulating a chemical attack, for good measure. This was to prepare us, they explained, for an appalling product, later to be known as Agent Orange, the incredible effectiveness of which had just been tested by the American warmongers ... At the time I regarded such assertions as propagandist hyperbole, not knowing that, years later, this brilliant invention would cause millions of deaths in Vietnam.

Walking along in the full heat of day made us perspire in bucketfuls. The eyepieces of my gas mask misted over – I had forgotten to smear them with a stick that protected the glass against humidity. After a shooting practice, during which I had been firing at a target more or less blindly, our section split up to follow routes that were due to join up again at the end of this asphyxia-inducing obstacle course.

I went off in my appointed direction, staggering like a drunkard and deafened by my own breathing through the respirator of the gas mask. After about half an hour, through the misted-up eyepieces, I caught sight of a river and the shadowy form of a willow ...

And a woman! Or at least a figure bent over the water, whose actions suggested the rinsing of linen. In the midst of the warlike madness in which I was a participant, her presence was eloquent of a humble and supreme truth, a means of escape.

I took several steps forward, the figure swayed in the fog of my vision and disappeared behind the foliage. I walked down to the water's edge and collapsed there, flinging my weapon to the ground and immediately tearing off my gas mask.

Once free from that oven, I remained for a moment doing nothing but drink in the air, with no thought for the military exercise whose course I had just strayed from. In front of me the river babbled its musical refrain, and the flower-decked braids of a plant floated there upon the water. This rippling motion, at the whim of the current, seemed to me to be endowed with a much deeper significance than that of our trek through forest thickets, firing at targets nailed to tree trunks . . .

A burst from a submachine gun rang out, bringing me back to reality, to this continuing simulation of post-atomic warfare. All around me the water was still repeating its melody, and the sun's radiance fractured into glittering scales before settling into a steady flow of sombre gold at a bend in the river. And the tops of the fir trees swayed in response to the great wind blowing in from the invisible ocean.

A few hundred yards away, men were advancing, clad in crude, all-enveloping rubbery garments, their heads moulded in thick latex. The air they breathed had an acrid smell to it, having passed through a filter. Their eyes, made hazy by the mist, saw neither the sky nor the transparency of the waters, only these targets: silhouettes fixed to trees, each with a red patch on the solar plexus, which must be riddled with bullets. There was a logic to this whole performance, for the enemy was preparing to incinerate this June forest in an atomic furnace. They had shown us a documentary film: areas of charred desert where two Japanese cities had once stood . . .

I pictured the woman who had just been alarmed by my extraterrestrial's outfit. She must now be following a forest trail, well away from this world gone mad. So, an escape from such a world must be possible!

No, I was not so naïve as to be one who proclaimed a gospel

of universal love. And yet the air I was breathing was the same as that on the other side of the ocean, and the lapping of the waters must sound the same on the islands of Japan or elsewhere. This moment in summer had the same serene resonance on every continent . . .

These notions helped me to remain calm when confronted by an officer who suddenly appeared behind me and addressed me with a brutal yell. I recognised him as Ratinsky, whom all the reservists detested – a young officer in the regular army, pompously aware of his rank. Blond, impeccably dressed in a uniform that had undoubtedly been taken in here and there by a dressmaker, he had always struck me as dangerous, on account of his relentless ambition. He used to repeat everything his superiors said, like a parrot, and was forever seeking to perform actions that would win their approval. That day he had an unhoped-for opportunity: a deserter taking his ease beside a stream, his submachine gun flung down on the grass and his special suit gaping wide. And all this in the middle of a nuclear bombardment.

He yelled at me without taking off his gas mask, then, realising that I could not make out much of what he was saying, took it off and emitted a belch, failing to conceal his relief at breathing fresh air. I studied him almost with compassion: a puny, blond fellow, foaming at the mouth with hatred, impatient to add another little star to his epaulettes.

Seeing that I was paying him scant attention, he raised his voice and began denigrating reservists, claiming that we had all forgotten how to load a rifle. This last sally woke me up. I picked up my submachine gun and explained in very measured tones: "The thing is, Comrade Sub-Lieutenant, when you're wearing a gas mask you can't see very well. So there's a great risk that, instead of aiming at the target, you aim at someone standing nearby. An involuntary error, an accident, you see. It can happen . . ." Ratinsky tensed, being not unaware that, on occasion, dictatorial officers were mown down in such "accidents". Unwilling to tempt fate, he snapped: "Right, Gartsev. You can repeat that to Captain Luskas. He'll make it clear to you what acts of insubordination result in."

Luskas, who was in charge of military security, was in quite a different league. A report written by him would suffice for any one of us to be arrested and sent to a camp. When he appeared on the scene, conversation faltered. Tall and bald, he had eyes of a brilliant blue like the crack in an ice floe. During the war he used to send "traitors" and "defeatists" to the firing squad. Nor had his mission changed very much since then . . . Believing that he served an idea, Luskas was intolerant of life's imperfections. If he had had the power to do so, he would have straightened out all the twisted tree trunks in the taiga that surrounded us.

I was expecting to be summoned before him, but the days passed and my misdemeanour seemed to have been forgotten. Until one moment when I passed him on the way to the canteen. Fixing me with his blue stare, he muttered: "So, Gartsev, let's say that was the dress rehearsal. But don't expect you'll be allowed a first night." And, adding nothing more, he moved on. I felt as if he had been reading my mind – a little while earlier I had been comparing the void that dwelled within me to the echoing of a voice in an empty theatre.

Being left in suspense like this was distressing, I wanted to talk about it to one of the rare comrades I could confide in. I had come across this sergeant, Mark Vassin, in the last days of the war and was struck by how at odds his great courage was with his very short stature. Seven years later we had met up again at this training area. He was a good deal older than me, but had nevertheless been called up – doubtless because he was a widower and had no children to look after.

I told him about the cryptic threat Luskas had uttered. Vassin smiled. "That reminds me of a funny story. An elderly examining magistrate who's sent lots of people to Siberia reaches retirement. His son takes over his files and comes upon the case of a plot against the Party. Within ten days he brings the investigation to a close and the 'conspirators' are shot. His father sighs: 'You poor idiot! That case paid my salary for ten years'..."

He stifled a laugh. "So I don't think our canny Captain Luskas will be in any great hurry to send you on holiday to Kolyma. Not as long as there are files like yours to keep him in business..."

I knew that Vassin himself had done time in a prison camp. "Nothing political," he would explain, "I just lost my temper."

Another of our exercises took the form of spending twenty-four hours in an underground shelter, without food, or water, while receiving a minimum of air from a narrow ventilation shaft and undergoing the effects of a series of explosions.

Each shelter could accommodate ten soldiers. I was about to enter the one allocated to my section, but Ratinsky held me back. "No, Gartsev, you're going into shelter number nineteen." I was not well placed to object. Number nineteen was small, almost abandoned, at any rate it had not once been used since our arrival. I was to remain alone there – Ratinsky had given careful thought to his revenge.

All the shelters had been constructed on the same model: a lining of thick planks deep down beneath six feet of earth – in fact a wooden house buried underground. Number nineteen was very cramped and, through lack of use, had turned into a great chest that smelled of rotting vegetation.

A coffin … The floor, spongy with damp, yielded underfoot. Once the heavy hatch was lowered into place the only source of illumination was one light bulb, which immediately began flickering. What was most astonishing was the abundance of roots, which, with their long, pale tresses, threaded their way across the ceiling, searching in the stagnant air for something to latch on to. I could not move a step without these braids clinging to my face. They also hung down from the ventilation shaft which, being blocked, was useless.

I was astounded by the diversity of the insects and worms that emerged from between the joins in the rotten timber. With revulsion, I set about brushing them off my low bed. But there were too many of them – it was as if in every crack there was a scaly or slimy multitude of them, spying on me before creeping into my clothing. Seething masses of them were also clustered along the trailing garlands of the roots and, more actively still, in the corner where the latrine ditch was located, covered with a rectangle of mouldy plywood.

I looked at my watch every couple of minutes, but the hands were stuck and making little headway.

At noon precisely there was an explosion and then, at one-minute intervals, two more. The clods of earth falling back onto the hatch evoked the sound of a train thundering along a railway track. And the more tangible effect was the creaking of the timbers which flung a whole new army of insects down onto me from the ceiling ...

Suddenly the light went out. They had forbidden us to carry matches and, besides, the tiniest flame would have rapidly used up the small amount of air available in that dungeon cell.

Disconcerted, I felt for that wretched light bulb and fiddled with it, but the socket, which was oxidised, disintegrated. My watch did not have a luminous dial, so I resigned myself to long hours of darkness. Spreading out my anti-atomic suit on the low bed, I lay down and tried to doze off...

It was the rhythm of my own breathing that woke me up. I was inhaling in little noisy jerks and the pulse in my temples was throbbing rapidly with a harsh echoing sound. I was short of air.

I leaped up towards the hatch and tried to raise it. It was doubtless covered with earth, deposited there by the explosion. Snatching up one of the planks from the low bed, I tried to knock it against this trapdoor. In the total darkness my blows went astray, scraping the ceiling, and deluged me with fragments of damp timber. I called out, giving the number of my shelter. And, very physically, I felt within myself the presence of a terrified homunculus, the "rag doll" – that compendium of my instinct for survival.

The darkness was suddenly tinged with iridescent circles, I swayed and felt myself going into a long, soundless fall.

The thin layer of still breathable air close to the ground caused me to come to. Stretched out on the rotten surface of the floor, I was inhaling with an uneven rhythm, as if at each gulp I was picking my way through the mouthfuls of now healthy, now polluted air that had accumulated at the bottom of this coffin. I would take a hundred breaths and then the iridescent circles in the darkness would return, giddiness, suffocation ...

With a fierce surge of energy for survival, I stood up and let out a shrill cry below the ventilation shaft clogged with roots. I gripped these with my fists and tugged at them, using the whole weight of my body ... I fell, dragging the strands I had thus torn out down on top of me, together with a cascade of earth, as well as fragments from filters that had long since crumbled. After a long moment when I hung in the balance between life and asphyxiation, a fine draught of air made its presence felt by a series of signs: the surface of the planks became a little colder, the bitter stench of decay became less intense and, best of all, regaining control of my reflexes, I managed to move my head to shake off the insects. As I lay there on the bed, it took me several minutes before I no longer had to make an effort to draw every breath. And now thirst was taking over from my fear of suffocation.

My return from the brink, instead of bringing me relief, weighed me down. So my momentary death had changed nothing! There I was, in the process of reintegrating my body, watching over its little whims and phobias. And the shock of having almost been buried alive, covered in vermin, yes, this very real simulation of my life's end, did not keep me from thinking again about Sveta, with a violent desire to win her back, to return to the routine of our carnal love.

Far from thrusting me up towards the lofty peaks of wisdom, that brief spell on the brink of non-existence, had, on the contrary, only amplified my very crass lust for life – to possess a woman, to go back to the old games of the human tribe. The "rag doll" was once more rampant within me!

I thought about the philosophers I had studied. The Greeks, the Romans, the mystics of the Middle Ages, Kant, Hegel and the inevitable Marx and Lenin . . . It seemed as if none of them had paid any heed to what was fundamental: the human core, that combination of animal and tribal elements which no supreme idea has been able to transcend, no Revolution has succeeded in bringing to heel.

All around us, in the prison camps that lay hidden in the taiga, thousands of tormented shadows inhabited barrack huts barely more comfortable than this shelter of mine. What course could a philosopher recommend to any of these prisoners? Resignation? Rebellion? Suicide? Or just the contemplation of an eventual return to . . . a free life? But what did this "freedom" consist of? Working, feeding yourself, amusing yourself, marrying, reproducing yourself? And also, from time to time, making war, dropping bombs, hating, killing, dying . . .

There was no wisdom that could give me an answer to this simplest of questions: how could we progress beyond bodies made for desire and brains designed for conquest in all the games of rivalry? What could be done about this cunning, cynical human animal, one that was never satisfied and whose existence was not so very different from that of the aggressive swarms of insects devouring one another in the cracks of my shelter? The "legitimacy of violence", as I called it in my thesis.

Suddenly a scratching noise could be heard that made me think it was a rat or some reptile. I stamped my foot, but the sound became even more substantial, then it was matched by a dull echo like an explosion. My thirst, ahead of my hearing, guessed it: thunder, rain . . .

Water!

The drops began falling, running down the ventilation shaft and those roots I had not succeeded in ripping out. In the darkness I located the garlands of them that were causing a thin trickle to run down.

If anyone could have seen me they would have thought I was kissing those long, tangled filaments. In fact, I was almost biting them, sucking in the water, as they absorbed it, and then spitting out sand and splinters of wood and charcoal from the disintegrated filters.

It probably took me a whole hour to quench my thirst and embark on scouring my face with those damp tresses. Reaching up with my arms, I grasped the air duct, tugged at it hard and fell to the ground, for the tube collapsed, coming away from the earth, and broke into several sections. Covered in mud, I sat up straight, remaining there beneath the opening that had just appeared.

My eyes, accustomed to the darkness, at once made out a pale glow. The rain had stopped, and the clear night sky was turning faintly blue. I could not see the moon through the gap but that was the source of this subtle radiance. A star seemed to be flickering among the tall grasses whose stems were swaying in the wind, out there, on the surface of the Earth, in a world which, seen from my tomb, was now so different.

I lingered there without stirring, my gaze bewitched by the incredible strangeness of the visible world. This gap above me opened out onto a life, compared with which, all I had lived through and learned so far was becoming unimportant. My disappointment in love and the doctrines that pretended to encompass the meaning of the universe. Such things found no echo in the truth I had just come close to. I gazed in wonderment to the point of giddiness at these grasses lightly brushing against a star. I even believed I had glimpsed a human shadow keeping watch. It was out there, beyond this earthy passage whose surface I could feel with my hand . . .

I would later realise that I had never before spent such a long time contemplating the night sky.

A fine shaft of sunlight woke me. I caught the sound of voices calling my name and, at the far end of the chimney, I recognised Ratinsky's face.

"Gartsev, can you hear me?" His words betrayed real uneasiness. I did not reply, I was still too remote from the whole performance that was about to begin all over again in their farcical human charade.

The sounds of spadework made me realise they were clearing the hatch, removing the earth thrown down by the explosions . . . I donned my anti-radiation suit and gas mask – not out of respect for orders, but rather as an ironic gesture to match the outcome of this exercise.

As I climbed back to the surface, I caught sight of Sub-Lieutenant Ratinsky, who had doubtless been afraid he might have to extract me from this ill-adapted shelter in a state of asphyxiation, in which case Captain Luskas, the spy hunter, would perceive it all as a conspiracy: if a soldier was done to death, was that just a device for tarnishing our army's image?

More than those two, it was the presence of Major Butov that amazed me. I came to attention in front of him and, still with a burlesque exaggeration that he chose to ignore, I mumbled: "Mission accomplished, Comrade Major." Almost sheepishly he growled, "Take off your gas mask, Gartsev . . ." I obeyed him and saw them all recoil: my face was black with mud and several strands of root clung to either side of my brow like the locks once sported by hussars.

"Who gave you the order to go into that shelter?" he asked me. His question was a mere formality, he was perfectly aware of who had allocated the tombs, but he preferred for me to name the guilty party. Ratinsky's eyes, little dark brown eyes, betrayed panic . . . I cleared my throat, spat out some grains of sand, and, once more, in a very correct posture, I made my report: "Comrade Major, I requested to undertake my training in shelter number nineteen to test my endurance. In atomic warfare many combatants could find themselves in conditions similar to those I've had to endure."

Butov nodded. "Very well, if you say so . . ." Plump and benevolent, he was not a man to go looking for trouble. "Go and wash, Gartsev. And stand down until 0900 hours tomorrow." He walked away, followed by Luskas.

Avoiding my eye, Ratinsky repeated, "Stand down . . ." and hurried off to catch up with his superiors.

I was proud not to have demeaned myself by denouncing him. But I knew it was a humane gesture he would not forgive. This was a recurring trait in his make-up and I was curious to test its inevitability.

Strangely enough, I felt partly responsible for what this man was. For I could find no way of explaining to him the life I had caught a glimpse of from the tomb in which he had interred me.

I should have been able to complete my three months of military service, caught between the farce of our world and the impossibility of speaking about those few moments that had so radically estranged me from it. I should have gone on emulating my fellow soldiers as they took part in this grotesque and lugubrious counterfeit version of the Third World War.

Yes, those simulations of atomic attacks would have continued in their tranquil course if, on the very next day, there had not been this alert.

III

SUMMONED EARLY IN THE MORNING TO THE COMMAND post, I found a small gathering of the initiated there: Luskas, Ratinsky, Vassin. And Butov, who addressed us. There was a note of unaccustomed concern in his voice. "The Commander of the military district has entrusted us with a mission of extreme importance ..."

He stubbed out his cigarette in an ashtray made from a shell case. Like the others, I anticipated one of two possibilities, both equally the stuff of probability and wild fantasy: either the Americans had launched a missile at Vladivostok or else we were in for a new exercise even more demented than the one involving my inhumation. This pair of alternatives speaks volumes about the rationality of the period we were living through.

"No, this is not about military manoeuvres," Butov resumed, guessing at our thoughts. "A very serious act has been committed in a nearby prison camp, fifteen miles from here. A criminal, armed and prepared to kill, has recently escaped ..." A note of justification could be heard in his voice. He turned to Luskas.

"He got away during a transfer, wounded a guard and stole

his rifle. And this is where it becomes a really vile business for us ... Yes, I know, Captain Luskas. According to the information just transmitted to me (and the communications were diabolical, as if by design), this prisoner, whose name is Lindholm or Lundholm, a foreign name, anyhow, unless that's the name of the place where he was born, well, after escaping, he found nothing better to do than to enter the perimeter of our training area here. I'd like to know what our sentries were doing! So you can understand now that it's not just a matter of lending a hand to the teams that have been sent out in pursuit of him, but also of cleansing a stain from the honour of our regiment."

He lit a fresh cigarette and growled, "Any questions?"

Neither Ratinsky, nor Vassin, nor, least of all, myself, dared to speak. Luskas surveyed us with his arctic-blue gaze and, instead of a question, issued an order, to make it clear that, while Butov would be in command, it would be under the supervision of himself, Luskas, as representative of military counter-espionage and guarantor of ideological purity. "All communication of anything regarding this to anyone at all," he barked, "is totally forbidden. Departure in twenty minutes ..." So as not to lose face, Butov muttered: "Move now!"

And so we set off, possessed of little information: after crossing the territory of our training area, an escaped prisoner with a Teutonic name was making his way through the taiga beside the river Amgun.

The urgent task was to cut off his path towards the north

where the terrain was even more desolate. His identity, apparently that of a foreigner, added a further gravity to our wild adventure. Was this an agent of the west, parachuted in to assist the Americans in launching an attack from their bases in Japan? Or even a former Nazi soldier, imprisoned in Siberia, trying to reach Japan, Hitler's former ally? At all events, the fact that Luskas had been attached to our group indicated that the dimension of espionage could not be ruled out.

Butov's presence was just as logical. He was the officer in command of the operation.

As for Ratinsky, it went without saying: in the eyes of this young officer our mission would be a dream opportunity to show off his talents, all the more so because the general staff had promised to reward success.

Mark Vassin had been judged indispensable because of his ability to control Almaz, the huge hound the prison camp authorities had loaned us, a cross between an Alsatian and a mastiff.

Thus everyone in our quintet knew what notes to play. Except me. To begin with, I hoped their decision to include me could be explained by contrition at having interred me in a shelter that had very nearly become my final resting place. I still had faith in the natural goodness of man . . .

One evening, as I found myself talking privately to Vassin, I told him about my amazement. "You know, Mark, I think your Almaz is ten times more useful than me. Why have they brought me along?" He called his dog over, took hold of his head and stroked him. Then he asked me: "Do you know that game, the fifth corner?" "Do you mean the game ruffians play?" I replied, amazed. "Sure. Four of them form a square and they put the fifth one in the middle. They all push him back so he can't get out . . ." Vassin nodded with a sigh. "I'm afraid if our little jaunt goes pear-shaped you may be the one that gets ejected from the square. I was talking to Ratinsky the other day and I sensed that was more or less their idea: you as a scapegoat, already with a black mark against you. The one Luskas could blame if things go wrong . . . So, watch out, Pavel."

I only half believed him. The beauty of the taiga was absorbing us into its slow, green, swaying rhythm, far removed from the spite of petty thoughts that might set us at one another's throats. After that spell in my anti-atomic tomb, I was now walking along feeling as if I could soar aloft towards the stained-glass window that was the sky framed by the branches of trees, and absorb the heady intoxication of the air, the vastness of the horizon and, above all, the wind that came from the ocean, connecting the tiniest needles of a cedar tree to that luminous infinity in which we were nothing. I filled my lungs to the point of giddiness, succumbing for a few seconds to a crazy hope: that the only purpose of our expedition might be this light, this impulse for freedom . . .

But immediately after this, with Luskas' eyes upon me, I was forced to stoop, searching the ground for clues left by the escaped prisoner as he passed, and sniffing the air so as to detect any smoke from a wood fire, yes, to remain faithful to the sleuthing objective of our mission. I obeyed orders, fulfilling my role of defaulter under surveillance, made to scurry here, there and everywhere, exploring this thicket, checking that detour . . .

And yet it was as early as the evening of the second day that I had a chance to disobey. The previous day Almaz had discovered footprints, clearly visible on a patch of mossy ground. Luskas urged us to move faster, no doubt counting on cornering the criminal before dusk fell. After a fruitless deviation I had just made on his orders, I was advancing at the rear of our Indian file. Suddenly, on a branch that overhung some barren marshland, I noticed a little bunch of yellow flowers attached to a twig. I almost called the others, then I thought better of it. Someone had signalled his passing in this way and I detected a certain subtlety in it: a mark on the ground would have been noticed at once by his pursuers, or trampled underfoot by animals. On the other hand, this little scrap of yellow, above my head, was only visible to someone who paused and looked upwards, embracing the brightness of the sky.

I caught up with the group and informed Luskas, "I've found nothing, Comrade Captain," secretly feeling that he and I were travelling on different roads.

AT NIGHT, FROM NOW ON, WE COULD SEE THE FIRES LIT by the escaped prisoner. He generally kept three of them going, a few yards apart, which made an effective attack impossible. It would have been easy to catch him asleep, but beside which fire? An assault on an armed man at night represented too great a risk. And the orders were strict: he must remain alive, so as to undergo an exemplary punishment designed to terrorise his fellow prisoners.

Then Luskas, who seemed to be in the greatest hurry to finish the whole thing, proposed that Almaz be let loose on the fugitive. Vassin opposed this with the calm firmness that I admired in him. "Comrade Captain, this fellow must be a good marksman. He'd kill the dog. Furthermore, he has a bayonet that he's stolen from his guard. Look at that cut there . . ." He pointed to the trunk of a dead birch tree that had been stripped with a blade to get at its white bark, so useful for lighting a quick fire. Luskas felt the tree with his hand. "That's something you could do with a pocket knife." "Maybe. But not this cut here," Vassin insisted. He plunged his index finger into a deep gash which showed the sturdiness of the blade. Lacking further arguments, Luskas emitted an icy little laugh. "Very well. If your Cerberus is afraid of getting a tiny scratch . . ." He hated being contradicted.

We resumed the chase, hoping the escaped prisoner would soon be overcome by fatigue. Butov expressed this with his customary geniality. "You'll see. One morning in three or four days' time we're going to pick this fellow up having a nap under a fir tree. We won't even have to fire a shot at him. Let's just wait a little . . ."

Behind his words I sensed something that we all, with the exception of Luskas, were feeling during this first stage of the chase. Once we had got into the way of it physically, it was not at all unpleasant to be forging a path through beautiful virgin forest, crossing streams where the water was as cool as a sorbet, forgetting the life we had left behind. This escapade of ours was a good deal more relaxing than those exercises designed to familiarise us with atomic warfare . . . It was only the tetchy presence of Luskas that kept us from surrendering to the enjoyable nature of this adventure.

The fugitive must have worked out our tactics. He had grasped that we needed to capture him alive and that the dog would not be let loose on him, and, above all, that none of us was in any hurry to expose himself to his bullets. He did not give the impression of wanting to outdistance us or to take refuge in some kind of hiding place, which would have been easy in among the hills and the mazes of waterways. No, he was following the course of the Amgun, sidestepping into the forest when patches of marshland made it impossible to walk along the bank, crossing little tributaries of the main river and, at night, choosing relatively exposed spots where we could not have approached him without being seen. As dusk fell and an increasingly inky darkness enveloped the taiga, the lights of his fires would make their appearance – luminous lures for anyone who might come to attack him.

"I'm sure he doesn't sleep there," Vassin said to me one evening.

I pictured a body rolled into a ball in the hollow of a rock, a fellow dressed in the worn garb of a prisoner, a man on the run, exhausted by the chase and with no hope of any help. A fugitive at bay, totally alone. In spite of myself, what I felt for him was not sympathy but rather that attraction which, from time immemorial, must always have created a bond between two solitary beings whose paths cross in a primeval forest.

The next morning Luskas woke us by barking: "Open your packs!"

We slept in two tents, one of which was shared by Butov and Luskas, the other by myself, Ratinsky and Vassin. It was the latter who, with great sangfroid, as ever, asked: "Comrade Captain, we open them ten times a day. What's going to be found there, apart from our gear and our tins of food?" Luskas fixed him with his steely look. "That's what I shall soon see, Sergeant Vassin. And I never forget anything I've seen or heard . . ."

With surprising dexterity, Ratinsky laid out the contents of his backpack, while I, for my part, daunted by my status as a suspect, made haste to demonstrate my innocence. Vassin followed suit, taking his time, as if to satisfy the whim of a child. Luskas inspected our belongings and then turned to Butov, as if the major should, quite naturally, have submitted to the same inspection.

Butov went rigid, like a bull on the point of charging, the red mounting to his neck. The face-off between them, which lasted a matter of seconds, made plain the mutual detestation felt by an army officer who had lived through battles under fire and a security supremo who spent his days ferreting about among the general staff. It would have been better if Luskas had had the insolence to insist on a search. Butov would have lost his temper and sent him packing, which would have liberated us from this sly oppressor. But Luskas remained silent, waiting for the other man to explode and make a remark that could be condemned politically . . .

Vassin deduced this and remarked in tones of good-natured curiosity: "Comrade Captain, tell us what you've mislaid. That'll make it easier to find it again . . ."

Luskas looked him up and down and hissed through gritted teeth, "I have not mislaid anything, Sergeant Vassin. Somebody has stolen my Zeiss binoculars." He lowered his voice and, as if to make us understand the gravity of the crime, added: "Which are equipped with non-reflective glass . . ." Vassin sighed, "Ah, non-reflective glass, that changes everything!" and threw me a quick, furtive smile.

Ratinsky grasped the opportunity to shine as a helpful sleuth. "Comrade Captain, when did you become aware of the

73

theft?" Generally imperturbable, Luskas seemed embarrassed. "Er . . . it was last night . . . Yes, I was up on a hill, making observations . . . And . . . I had an emergency. I hung the glasses on a tree. Then . . . well, I did what I had to do. And when I'd finished, the glasses had gone. But I only became aware of it this morning . . ."

Butov's revenge was bang on target. "The next time you have an emergency, Captain, I mean the urge to defecate on a hilltop, I'll detail Gartsev to mount guard under the tree where you like to hang up your spyglass on such occasions. And now, if you think we want to be lumbered with a day's march going back to look for your pretty toy, don't count on us!"

Luskas glared at him with hatred but made no reply . . .

That night I was on guard, and when Vassin relieved me at midnight he quietly told me: "Do you know something? He didn't leave his binoculars behind at all. I saw him at the camp last night, just before turning in and he still had them. He was taking a look at the escaped prisoner's fires . . . So somebody must have pinched them while he was asleep. But who?"

The disappearance of the captain's "toy" ought to have made our pursuit more difficult, but the fugitive did not become harder to spot and the distance separating us did not increase. The only consequence of this theft was of a more comic nature: every time Luskas stepped aside for an "emergency", I exchanged knowing glances with Vassin and mimed standing to attention beneath the tree where the captain was answering a call of nature.

*

Occasions when we could relax became rare. Sensing himself to be the object of ridicule, Luskas fumed and forced us to embark on encircling manoeuvres that were as exhausting as they were futile, and at night made us mount guard in pairs and even, on occasion, ordered me to crawl towards the fugitive, "to harrass him and deprive him of sleep".

On the sixth day Butov, scarlet with rage, bellowed: "Now look here, Captain, you're beginning to get on our tits! Do you understand?"

Luskas gave a little unexpected smile, as thin as a knife blade. "I understand you very well, Comrade Major. I shall make a note of it in my report."

The word was out, plunging us all into silence. A report in which the fate of each one of us could be sealed in a single paragraph: blame, dishonourable discharge, prison. Butov drew a mighty breath and chewed his lip, like an animal on a leash which has just been shortened. As he often did, Vassin sought to ease the tension.

"Comrade Captain, may I draw your attention to something strange that concerns me? It's this . . . We've been on the trail of this escapee for a week now and he's never too far away and never too close. We can see him. But we're seeing him without seeing him . . ."

"What are you driving at, Sergeant?"

"It's one of two things. Either he's very weak and can't manage to shake us off. After all, at the moment of his escape he might have sprained an ankle . . . Or else he's very strong and then . . ."

"And then what? He's enjoying himself giving us a tour of the taiga? Your theory doesn't stand up, Sergeant. 'Never too far, never too close . . .' That's all totally irrelevant. We have one objective: to arrest a criminal. Full stop. Very early tomorrow morning, when he's fast asleep, we will attempt to apprehend him. Vassin, you will lead the advance with the dog. Ratinsky, you will go next, following the course of the river, and the rest of us will remain in the rear to cut off his escape. Reveille at 0300 hours."

That night, on guard with Vassin, I rebuked him gently. "I know you meant well with your theories, Mark. But Luskas has just used them to saddle us with this stupid operation that's going to finish us all off. Besides, I don't understand. Do you really think the prisoner's playing games with us?"

Seated in front of the fire, he threw some leafy branches into the flames. They did not burn very well, but gave off thick smoke to protect us from the mosquitoes.

"I think he's a very intelligent fellow. If he'd wanted to get away from us he'd have done so long ago."

"But if he's so clever, why would he go through all this rigmarole?"

"This 'rigmarole' could save his life. Think about it, Pavel. If he'd totally given us the slip the very first day we'd have gone back empty-handed and the top brass would have started a new hunt with several teams of men and maybe even a helicopter. And they'd have caught him. On the other hand, as long as we don't return, the prison camp authorities think we're likely to bring him back any day now . . . And time is on his side."

"What you're saying makes sense. But why haven't you explained this to Luskas?"

Vassin replied with a dull cough and thrust another armful onto the fire. Then he looked at me with anguished intensity.

"Because I understand him, this fugitive. In the camp where I spent four years, I dreamed of escaping a hundred times. I didn't do it. He has dared to. If we have to nab him, then we will. We're in the army. After all, he may be a murderer. But if I learn that he's a political prisoner, well then, Luskas will find it hard to persuade me ..."

He turned and patted the dog that lay sleeping in the shadows beside him. "He's a bit weary, my Almaz. And he eats too much. I don't know how he manages to catch all this game. Look at this capercaillie."

I picked up the half-eaten bird, surprised to see a cluster of herbs spilling out of its innards. I was going to ask Vassin about this when the snap of a twig put us on our guard. Ratinsky appeared, not coming from the tents, but climbing up from the riverbank. "You'd do better to remain on the alert, instead of gossiping," he snapped briskly before disappearing.

I sensed my own fear in Vassin's look. "Did he hear us talking about the political prisoner? And, if so, will he denounce us to Luskas?"

Once again I felt a shudder of cowardice within me: there it was, that "rag doll", counselling obedience, the suppression of any rash remarks, the exclusion of everything that made us truly alive.

WE APPROACHED THE ESCAPED PRISONER'S CAMP IN the darkness, closer than within rifle range. Through the tangled branches it was possible to see three clusters of embers that more or less indicated the whereabouts of the man. The fires were certainly decoys, the fugitive spending the night away from them. Nevertheless, after a minute's scrutiny ("if only I had my binoculars," muttered Luskas), we finally made out a dark shape lying at the centre of the triangle. "That's him," hissed Ratinsky. "Now the main thing is not to wake him . . ."

We advanced in a tight line. Occasionally the dog emitted barely audible groans.

Some fifty yards from our goal a minor river barred our way. By the first pale light of dawn we could see the fires better and, beneath a rocky overhang, the cocoon of the escaped prisoner, still unmoving. In silence Ratinsky raised his rifle, indicating the sleeping man with a movement of his chin. We grasped the idea: to wound the prisoner, thus depriving him of all possibility of resistance. Luskas shook his head vehemently, forbidding this: it was difficult to aim accurately in the darkness. As for dragging a corpse through the taiga, that would have been too tough a task. And, above all, the governor of the prison camp demanded a captive fully alive, capable of speaking under torture and of being executed in an exemplary fashion.

The riverbanks were steep and the current appeared very swift. Luskas indicated to me that I should go downstream and look for a ford, but at the same moment Vassin, being pulled along by Almaz, discovered another way across: two tree trunks with the branches lopped off, lying close together, side by side, to form a narrow bridge. Jabbing the air with his forefinger in the absence of words, Luskas explained the plan of attack to us: Ratinsky would cross first, followed by Butov. When they reached the camp they would rush at the fugitive, while he, Luskas, would cut off any possible escape towards the rocks. I was to stand guard over the entrance to the bridge – and also, while I was at it, over our kit, which would be too cumbersome to take on the attack. Vassin, with the dog, would patrol the river, as the escaped prisoner might seek to get away by swimming . . .

At the end of this briefing Butov scowled, pushed Ratinsky aside and set off in front. Luskas disregarded this deviation.

The thinking behind his plan was clear: Butov and Ratinsky would lay hands on the criminal and he, Luskas, would return in triumph. My supporting role was minimal, but, if the occasion demanded, I could be blamed for any failure. Vassin, patrolling the riverbank, had a scarcely better part to play than me . . .

Butov, Ratinsky and Luskas inched forward slowly, testing the solidity of the structure with their feet. Each of them was carrying his rifle like a tightrope walker's pole. The tree trunks, long and massive, did not look as if they were shifting under their weight.

I reflected that the assault was either going to lead to violent hand to hand fighting, or to the limp surrender of a man at the end of his tether, relieved at not having to fight. Instinctively, and with warmth, I found myself wishing the latter outcome for him, and when I asked myself why, it was, oddly, the memory of that posy of yellow flowers dangling from a branch that came back to me, that frail emblem of his dash for freedom . . .

Butov was almost at the far end of the bridge when suddenly he gave a start, let fly an oath and stamped hard on the tree trunk as if crushing a snake. Ratinsky backed away, trying to avoid this large, teetering body, but was struck by Butov's rifle. They fell into the fast-flowing river together. At first Luskas resisted the shaking motion, but then, poised above the void, waving his arms wildly, he, too, fell, though less chaotically than the others. Disappearing into the whirling current, they all resurfaced twenty yards downstream, struggling, hanging on to a rock here, a branch there . . .

Vassin and I caught up with them on a sandy beach at a place where the river broadened out and could be forded. Where we should have crossed . . . Butov was still swearing, cursing the "bloody larch" that had given way under his weight. Ratinsky was pacing up and down on the bank in the hope of retrieving the rifles. Luskas was feverishly checking the maps and documents in his pack . . .

We climbed up to the escaped prisoner's camp without

really counting on a further sight of him there. The fires had gone out and the cocoon we had taken for a body lying there consisted of fir branches, arranged to simulate the figure of a sleeping man ... The secret of the bridge was easy to explain: the far end of it had been balanced across two smooth boulders in such a way as to cause the tree trunks to slip once a foot was placed on this seesaw. It was a trap, simple and hard to detect. But one that I should have detected!

Luskas declared this in stinging tones. "I ordered you to secure a safe route for us. It was your duty to eliminate the possibility of an accident ..." As I listened to him, I realised that Vassin was right: all setbacks would be blamed on me because that was the role assigned to me in our cast of characters. Above all, I understood that such barely justified accusations indicated that Luskas was beginning to lose control of things. He was aware of this himself and, containing his anger, ordered: "To compensate for that serious error, you would be well advised to recover the rifles lost through your negligence."

I dived into the torrent a dozen times. The water was icy, the current very fast and, in this narrow stretch lined with rocks, it was at least twelve feet deep. Vassin held me on a length of rope, which he hauled on, to help me climb out. He had built a great bonfire so that the shipwrecked mariners could dry their clothes and I could warm myself after each attempt. Listening to Luskas' directions, I was shaking with cold: sound out the river closer to the shore; try round behind a sunken tree; probe a cleft in the rock ... The rifles could not be found. I would have needed proper diving equipment.

In the end, even the flames could no longer calm my shivering. Butov, who had just put his uniform, now fully dry, back on again, called out: "All right, Gartsev. You can stop now. We're not going to get them back. Come and warm yourself!" Luskas thrust out his chin, preparing to countermand the order, but Vassin got there first. "Comrade Captain, if Gartsev fell ill that would slow us down badly. We still have two rifles and three revolvers. That should certainly be enough to arrest the criminal."

Doing little to conceal a note of malicious glee, Luskas replied: "That may well be so, Sergeant. So long as we all really want to arrest him. Even if he turns out to be what some people call a 'political' prisoner."

That night I was on guard with Vassin. There was a somewhat bitter scent borne in on the wind that made us aware of the far distant presence of the ocean.

"If you headed north," Vassin remarked softly, "you'd reach the coast within three or four days . . ." He inhaled deeply with closed eyes and I thought I could see what he was picturing – the taiga growing brighter, filling with light and suddenly opening out onto the mists of an endless space, one where all griefs and fears vanish. One fear in particular: Ratinsky had overheard our conversation the previous night, that incautious remark about the political prisoner, and had denounced us to Luskas . . . Those words of ours could be portrayed as an attack on the security of the State, all it would take would be for a cunningly crafted accusation to be put on file.

We knew this. But the breeze coming from the Pacific made such a threat seem vague, immaterial . . . Sotto voce, Vassin called out into the night: "Hey, Ratinsky, you little sneak! Which fir tree are you hiding behind? Come over here instead of catching your death out there in the dark!" Naturally there was no reply, but this childish behaviour reflected a whole new sense of liberation: the feeling that it would be possible to get up and start walking towards the north, with no other goal than the source of this cool, bitter air, over there, the ocean, alive and eternal . . .

Vassin shook his head, emerging from this dream which, for the first time, did not seem completely fanciful to us.

"He's always drowsy, my Almaz," sighed Vassin, stroking the sleeping dog's back.

"He must be exhausted with all that running around from dawn to dusk."

"No, he's not tired," objected Vassin. "You remember how I told you he's managed to catch a lot of game . . . And he's not a hunting dog!"

"So how does he do it?"

"Someone gives it to him. Yes, they do. Sometimes Almaz finds a partridge on the trail, sometimes a hare . . ."

"Hold on . . . Do you mean that . . . the fugitive is feeding him?"

"Yes. Or rather, he's neutralising him. Look at this herb that he stuffs into his gifts. The people in these parts call it *dremnik*, the sleeping herb. They make infusions from it . . ."

"But how does this fellow manage to shoot all the game?"

"He sets traps. A bit like with that bridge. Rather more subtle devices, of course. Wild creatures are not as stupid as us."

He smiled and in a sudden real surge of affection laid his cheek against the dog's muzzle. "Sleep on, Almaz. It's better than going and ripping apart that poor guy who's trying to escape..."

Without my knowing it, that embrace and the sadness in Vassin's voice would stick in my memory. With the sixth sense that forms a bond between us and beings we are fond of, he must have had a premonition of the fate that awaited his dog.

THE NEXT MORNING LUSKAS ORDERED ME TO CLIMB UP onto some high ground that overlooked our camp and give him the most detailed report possible on the topography of the terrain. A meaningless phrase, he knew, but, as the leadership of this jaunt of ours was slipping from his grasp, he was putting on airs as a master strategist.

This hillside, covered as it was in the dwarf pine trees of a stlanik, held out the prospect of an arduous ascent and I decided to take my time. Luskas was quite capable of making me retrace my footsteps, as had happened before, saying that altered circumstances had made my mission unnecessary . . .

Halfway through my climb I stopped to catch my breath. I was looking out over the dense taiga, this immeasurable stretch of land covered in vegetation. Seen from on high it was the colours, green, grey, olive, purple, that best showed the contours of it, forming curves, stripes, alternation between patches of shadow and areas of light. And yet this broad expanse, with no sight of any coastline, stretched all the way to the horizon, quite uninterrupted. It was only threaded through here and there by the sinuous glitter of tributaries of the Amgun.

I was in the process of taking note of "the topography of the terrain" when, quite close to me, a branch stirred and the silence that followed seemed to me more complete than it had been before. Was this caused by my holding my breath or by the motionlessness of the animal that had just given itself away? This moment of stillness gave me a better sense of the depth of the forest, in which these two beings were present in such close proximity; myself and this animal . . . Or this man?

After a minute had passed I loaded my rifle and moved forward, trying to melt into this low forest where the trees were rarely taller than I was. What animal could be lurking in the depths of this seething mass of conifers? A lynx? A bear? Or that even rarer carnivore, an ounce, the snow leopard that Butov spoke of hunting, a cunning feline that can leap as far as eight yards. Or even a tiger from the banks of the Usuri. But did these animals come as far north as this region, as far as the Amgun?

I knew that wild creatures avoided encounters and I was certain that the flight of one of them among these low pine trees would have been easy to detect. Yet nothing stirred. So it could be a man. The only man who was of interest to me!

I forgot the pity I had managed to feel for the escaped prisoner. This was too good an opportunity to catch him and hand him over to the others, above all to Luskas. Such a trophy would rehabilitate me for good! To arrest this criminal, to be rewarded, decorated, to add lustre to my life with a heroic deed. To go back to the reassuring routine of the games all human beings play. To see Sveta again . . . These ideas, all jumbled together, set off a wild throbbing that pounded in my temples. I was ready to crush the man's face into the ground, to stop him breathing...

Threading my way between the trees, I emerged into a clearing. And before grasping what it was I saw, I almost opened fire.

There was a grey smock hung from some branches and its sleeves were swaying. The worn fabric had a long tear in it. Taking a step forward, I could make out stitches and a broad needle hanging from a thread. Suddenly I sensed that I was being watched. An instinctive feeling, impossible to prove, but I was sure of it. A gaze held me rooted to the spot, depriving me of all will. I pictured a rifle taking aim at me, or more likely a bayonet sliding across my throat.

Like a spinning top thrown off balance, I began pivoting to the left and to the right, trying to glimpse what was hidden behind my back, pointing my gun at my own shadow, getting my feet caught up in tree roots and not even aware that I was whispering feverishly all the while – a confused string of threats directed at an invisible enemy.

I came back down the slope with that frantic whirling motion, convinced I must protect the precious "rag doll" within me, that personification of all my hopes of happiness. It was this that made me fearful, cowardly, ready to tell Luskas everything.

My report was being composed to the rhythm of my strides: "Comrade Captain, at this very moment the prisoner's moving through this stlanik. We need to launch an immediate drive!"

A voice called out to me while I was still a long way from our camp. It was Luskas and it was as though he had been waiting for me among the trees.

"So, Gartsev, what have you seen?"

My throat became constricted. "Comrade Captain ... I've ..." The vision of a smock with a half-mended tear in it came back to me. The prisoner's grey smock. A man exhausted, bare-chested, hiding in the thicket ...

"I've not seen anything, Comrade Captain ... The tributary we'll need to cross is about a couple of miles from here ..."

Luskas fixed me with his steely blue stare and, instead of his usual contempt, I thought I glimpsed in it a brief moment of disarray. He pulled himself together, resuming his customary tones of malevolent arrogance. "So, do I understand correctly? You've seen nothing? No trace of anything?"

The idea that he could have been following close behind me – and seen what I had seen – took my breath away. But again, with a feeling of relief that was both desperate and exhila-rating, I repeated in more resolute tones: "No, nothing, Comrade Captain. The escaped prisoner must be exhausted and I reckon he's avoiding high ground."

Back at the camp Luskas summoned Vassin. "Sergeant, as our scout –" he indicated me with his chin – "has found nothing suspicious, you will unleash the dog ... I'm telling you – you will unleash the dog. No 'ifs' or 'buts', that's an order."

For the rest of the day Luskas did not address another word to me and his silence seemed to indicate that I had been found guilty: as if he had followed me up the hill, had seen the grey smock ... The "rag doll" quaked within me, infecting me with its dread. To rid myself of this, I imagined the prisoner stealing back to his garment, removing the needle and putting the smock on again . . . Strangely enough, this mental picture gave me a powerful feeling of release.

THE ESCAPED PRISONER DID NOT CHANGE COURSE, continued beside the Amgun, located a ford on one of its tributaries and then returned once more to the bank of the main river. The sun was grazing the tops of the trees when Almaz became excited, sniffing the ground with a hunter's zest. Vassin was obliged to trot along behind him, Ratinsky took aim with his rifle at a hypothetical target close at hand. Luskas held back from running, but the prospect of an imminent capture was making him visibly excited.

"They're dividing up the proverbial bear's skin already . . ." muttered Butov, who, given his corpulence, was finding it difficult to keep up this speed of advance. The bear's skin . . . He did not know how close to the mark he was. To justify his slow pace, he said to me, "Listen, Gartsev, we'll bring up the rear to cut this fellow off, in case the dog drives him back towards us. But the fact is, it would take a whole troop to corner him. The man's not a novice . . . Wait a moment, I've got something to sort out."

I saw him move off towards a little stream and squat down behind a bush. I looked away so as not to embarrass him. The team giving chase were about a hundred yards ahead of us now, and again I pictured the prisoner clad in his torn smock, a man around whom the noose of the hunt was drawing tighter.

Butov reappeared, looking more relaxed, his face now glowing pink. "Good. Off we go, Gartsev. Life is beautiful and . . . what was it Gorky said? Yes, that's it, beautiful and full of surprises!"

I detected a hint of something piquant and volatile on his breath, but alcohol did not occur to me, because getting hold of it here seemed unthinkable. His good mood made me almost happy: there we were walking along in the middle of a forest made fragrant with the scent of resin, the sky was cloudless, it was not too hot and our halt for the evening was close at hand.

The first gunshot took us by surprise. Butov looked at me, as if to see if I had heard the same thing. But a fresh shot rang out, with multiple echoes, then another and another . . . We started to run.

Reaching the spot before Butov, I saw Ratinsky brandishing his rifle like a spear and shouting at the top of his voice: "It was a bear! I've killed a bear! In fact, two, I think. Over there, they're over there!"

He set off down a pathway and we followed him. Luskas drew his revolver. Butov, as he caught up with us, did the same. I was also preparing to fire. Not one bear, but two! Possibly merely wounded and therefore doubly dangerous . . .

We made our way down to a silted-up watercourse and saw a dark mass, hidden amid the ferns. The creature did not seem very impressive to me. A bear cub? Vassin went over to it and lifted up one of its legs with the toe of his boot. It fell back limply.

"You've shot a wolverine, Comrade Sub-Lieutenant," he remarked gravely, with barely concealed irony. "A fine male."

As if to avoid being too cruel to this idiot, Ratinsky, he added: "At a distance the wolverine looks like a bear. The same muzzle, the same gait . . . And what about the second one? No doubt that was its mate . . ."

We walked along beside the stream and suddenly, thrusting everyone aside, Vassin raced through the undergrowth. I heard his dull cry, then a violent groan, one of a sorrow whose full intensity had not yet been plumbed.

We found him kneeling among some Labrador tea bushes, his cheek pressed against the chest of another animal. Convinced, as we were, that what lay before us was another wolverine, it took us a few seconds to realise that it was Almaz.

Vassin stood up, took a step towards Ratinsky and, without a word, struck him full in the face. The sub-lieutenant grabbed at the branches of a tree and saved himself from falling. The rifle dropped from his grasp. He stood up straight and spluttered with indignation: "You'll be court-martialled for this . . . You'll end up rotting in a camp." And he began drawing his revolver. At that moment Butov arrived on the scene and his voice snapped out with threatening authority: "Lower your gun, Sub-Lieutenant!"

Ratinsky obeyed, but it was Luskas who hastened to add: "Sergeant Vassin, you're under arrest. Hand over your weapon!"

The weapon, the rifle with its now empty magazine, lay at Ratinsky's feet. As for Vassin, he did not seem to have heard anything. Going back to the dog, he knelt down once more, trying to staunch the blood flowing from Almaz's chest. He seemed distracted, indifferent to what might happen to him.

"Tonight you will bind his hands and feet," Luskas ordered me. Vassin stood up and went over to Butov. I thought he was going to demand that the punishment be revoked, but he asked: "Comrade Major, may I have permission to bury the dog?" Butov nodded, then turned to us and declared, "Come along, we must get back to the Amgun ..."

I saw Vassin carrying Almaz over to a sandy slope beside the stream ... He met up with us again at the camp, where Ratinsky had thoughtfully prepared two lengths of cord.

That night, as I was "guarding" Vassin, I freed him from his bonds and sought to restore the light and friendly tone of our night-time conversations. He barely replied, lapsing back into a heavy silence from which I struggled to draw him out.

"He's thinking about his dog," I said to myself, surprised by the depth of his distress, which seemed disproportionate. Especially since he had just now, a little unwillingly, conceded: "Losing Almaz is one thing. But . . . Ratinsky would have fired like that at the prisoner. In his eyes, there's not much difference ..."

These words of his gave me a way of bringing him out of his withdrawal into himself. "That's just it, Mark. You should think about what would have happened to Almaz on our return. Back with the screws at the camp he'd have spent the rest of his life barking at the prisoners, and at every escape attempt sinking his fangs into their throats! At least he's had a good life for these last few days. Out in the wild and not behind barbed wire. And he hasn't harmed a soul!"

Vassin shook his head, and the two of us looked at the three glowing spots poised in the darkness, the fires lit by the fugitive a thousand yards from our camp.

"For me, that dog, you see, Pavel . . . I don't have many ties left in my life . . ."

His voice grew lighter – my arguments must have comforted him. No ties . . . Like that escaped prisoner in the night.

Ratinsky arrived to relieve me, noticed the cords had been removed and ordered me to put everything back in place. I fastened them as loosely as possible. Vassin gave a little smile, and whispered, "There they are, my ties . . ."

IN THE END LUSKAS BEGAN ISSUING ORDERS THAT LOST all coherence. He no longer sought to conceal his confusion. And also his fear. Vassin had mentioned this to me several days earlier. "He's off his rocker now, our spycatcher. I think he's simply got the wind up. He's a townie and I don't suppose he feels at home coming face to face with the taiga ..."

I remembered that at the moment when Ratinsky had flushed out the two "bears", Luskas had hung back, ready to cut and run. Amid all the shouting and the gunfire his cowardice had passed unnoticed ...

One night he roused us well before dawn and, as if challenging us to protest, declared: "You'll have your breakfast when the mission's completed!" Ratinsky came bounding up, eager to impress the person he depended on for his promotion. Vassin and I could not allow ourselves the luxury of a rebellion. But Butov rolled over in bed and growled: "You'd better take a few wine corks with you, Captain. Why? Because this fellow's going to take pot shots at you, fore and aft. You can stop up the holes with them. And now why don't you just bugger off with your idiotic offensives! Napoleon Bonaparte, my arse ..."

As we left, we heard him snoring. He was no longer trying to hide his loathing for Luskas.

We spent more than an hour feeling our way in the darkness, alarming animals that took to their heels, leaving us more scared than they were. On several occasions Ratinsky, armed with the rifle confiscated from Vassin, almost fired at their shadows. Luskas, for his part, walked along gripping his revolver, in the foolish hope of coming upon the escaped prisoner very close to our path.

What was most surprising was that his calculation that night proved to be effective. Our tactic was so incongruous that the prisoner could not have foreseen the possibility of it. When we reached his campfires it was as if he had just fled, without having time to take with him the two plump salmon that were in the latter stages of being smoked on a grill made of small branches . . .

The day was just beginning to dawn and we had a clear view of him among the pine trees that covered the side of a valley. He was walking fast, but not running. His back was hidden beneath an odd kind of knapsack, visibly fashioned from a piece of canvas. Not very tall, of somewhat slight stature, he wore a big hood that concealed his head. He carried his rifle horizontally, with the trigger uppermost, so that he could fire behind him without turning round and taking aim.

"He's limping a little," Vassin said softly. "His boots must be in shreds . . ." The note of sympathy I was aware of in his words seemed to confirm the inevitable: the man could no longer escape us. He was enjoying his last minutes of freedom.

He found himself trapped crossing a river. As we came down the bank, we could see him up to his neck in the water, in among the willows that grew on the far shore. Their branches were keeping him from climbing out, catapulting him back into the current, which was very powerful at this point. Struggling against the tangle of twigs, he missed his footing, then clung onto a more solid branch . . . From time to time he was hidden from us by a cloud of mist. Then in the murky haze before the day dawned the shaking of the branches gave him away. His hood made a target that was easy to distinguish.

That was what Ratinsky must have said to himself, as he took aim at it. I threw an anxious glance at Luskas, expecting him to voice a reminder of our orders: the escaped prisoner must remain alive. But the captain did not bat an eyelid. Ratinsky aimed, was starting to press the trigger . . .

I rushed at him with a shout: "Stop! We mustn't kill him!" I barged into him, he swore, thrust me away with the butt of his rifle, took up position again and fired. The hooded head amid the branches quivered, then froze. At the same time as me, Vassin yelled: "Captain! The order was not to shoot him!"

Luskas replied calmly: "That's correct. But the criminal attacked us, putting our lives in danger. The sub-lieutenant was compelled to act in legitimate self-defence. We shall cross by the ford and retrieve the body. Move now!"

We realised that this "legitimate self-defence" would be the version Luskas would report to the authorities.

Ratinsky went into the water, eager to display his prey in

front of his superior officer. I remembered having experienced that same animal glee on the hillside where I found the prisoner's smock . . . Yes, I, too, had seen that as a trophy.

Now he had been killed the man had become something quite different for me, not on account of his death, but because I had seen him walking along a little while before: a slim figure, with no resemblance to the hefty jailbird we had been picturing.

The fog was growing thicker and it was from the depths of its cotton wool density that Ratinsky's exclamation emerged. "I can't find the body!"

We went over to him, parting the screen of willow. He was emerging from the water, naked, shivering with cold and brandishing a waterlogged piece of fabric.

"It's his hood," he explained. "But where's the body? I'll go and look further downstream. It'll come to the surface, I'm sure of it . . ."

Luskas, equally baffled, paced along, following the direction of the current, and suddenly, with an unguarded candour that was unusual in him, let out a yelp. "But what's this? Whose are these? Gartsev, did you come this way?"

I saw some footprints that led towards the forest. Putting my boot down beside one of them, I could see that my foot was much longer than the print left by the escaped prisoner. Vassin joined us and repeated the test, with the same result. Ratinsky, who was shivering beside the fire he had just lit, asked: "So, can you see the body?"

At this moment Butov caught up with us. With a glance at Ratinsky and then at the fugitive's footprints, he took in the situation. "The body's still on the run. Cover your genitals, Sub-Lieutenant. Mosquito bites can give you a hard-on."

The fugitive's trick was certainly a clever one, attaching his hood to a branch, diving in, and climbing out onto the bank a few yards further down, screened by the undergrowth, but it was a desperate expedient, a last-ditch stand.

"Did you see his footprints?" Vassin asked softly. "You can see the marks of his toes. He's almost going barefoot . . ."

Still more serious for him was the fact that we now knew who he was. Not some formidable trapper but a person like ourselves, dressed in worn rags, a man of quite modest stature who, each time he unveiled another of his tricks, was teaching them to us, one by one.

The real hunt was now on, a drive at close quarters, of the kind that arouses the predator's instinct in man.

We stamped out the fire and set off at once. The fugitive must also have taken some time to warm himself, having waded in fully dressed. At the spot where he had just made a brief halt the embers were still warm, and in the grass, silvered with dew, dark traces showed that someone had very recently passed that way . . . We ate without calling a halt, eager to maintain a pace that he could no longer keep up. The thrill of the chase, the closeness of the quarry, all this spurred me on and suppressed any thoughts about this man's extreme weakness.

Only once did the cruelty of our headlong pursuit cross my mind again. The fugitive's tracks passed over some flat, chalky rocks. And it was on the surface of one of them that Vassin showed me a footprint – a trace partly coloured red. Blood . . .

Despite his exhaustion, the fugitive managed to hold out until nightfall. We had to call a halt to our drive in order to identify the place where he was stopping and pitch our tents.

Never, since the start of our expedition, had we spent the night so close to the spot where the fugitive was camping. He lit only a single fire, no longer having the strength to prepare all his luminous decoys.

I was on guard, feeding the flames from time to time. As I was beginning to doze off, a heavy footstep alerted me. A figure was lurching about beside our two tents. I picked up my rifle . . .

It was Butov, stooped and grumbling furiously. He flopped down beside the fire, took out a large, slightly bent cigarette, lit it from a brand, and inhaled deeply. And spoke, adopting softer tones than those of the officer giving orders.

"That damned Luskas! He keeps me awake! He's forever talking drivel in his sleep! He rambles on and on . . ."

During my times on guard I had occasionally heard conversations coming from their tent and found it surprising: the mutual hatred of those two men was barely camouflaged and they had little to say to one another.

Giving way to my curiosity, I remarked quietly, as if thinking aloud: "Oh, I thought you were discussing plans for our operation with the captain . . ."

Butov wagged his forefinger in negation.

"It's always him that's talking. He keeps repeating the same rubbish . . ."

"Rubbish?"

"Worse than that. The ravings of a lunatic. Especially when he starts shouting. He shouts in whispers! It's enough to make your blood run cold. What does he shout? Names. Then bits of official rigmarole. Things like: 'In accordance with article such and such of the penal code . . .' That comes from his old trade . . . And then all of a sudden . . . Well then, it's better not to hear him. He seems to be blubbing, mumbling the same thing over and over again. 'Their necks are looking at me . . . The backs of their necks are looking at me . . .'"

Butov gave me a slightly sheepish glance, then, deciding not to hide it any longer, took a flask out of his pocket, unscrewed the top, drank a draught and gave a long noisy exhalation.

"Would you like a drop, Gartsev?"

Respecting my refusal ("I'm on guard, Comrade Major . . ."), he breathed hard, to ease the burning from the spirit, then went on with his tale.

"Yes, it's his past that hounds him. A bit like us chasing after that little jailbird. During the war Luskas took part in the struggle against 'defeatists' and 'ideologically hostile elements', as they used to say at the time. Often good officers. He shot hundreds! Quick as a flash, he'd single out an enemy and, hey presto, the firing squad! With no other form of trial. I used to come across types who were doing the same filthy job as him. Some of them, and it must have been how it was with Luskas, preferred killing a man with their service revolver. A matter of taste. One bullet in the back of the neck and the case is closed. Except, you see, Gartsev, even if he shot them in the back of the neck, before he did so, he couldn't avoid seeing the looks in all those soldiers' eyes. And now, in his dreams, their looks come back to him. He fires, the necks are shattered, but their eyes bore into him. And he yells. Those eyes will follow him until the day he dies. And maybe after that as well . . ."

He took another drink but instead of uttering a sigh of relief, grew tense, cocked an ear, signing to me not to move. In the darkness the rustling of footsteps lasted for a few seconds, then, responding to our silence, faded away. Butov leaned towards me and whispered: "It's that sneak Ratinsky on the prowl . . . He's another one who'll end up having dreams filled with men's eyes, calling him to account . . ."

No longer lowering his voice, he growled: "Go and get a bit of sleep, Gartsev. I'll look after the fire."

IN THE MORNING WE WATCHED THE ESCAPED PRISONER striking camp: we had never witnessed this before. Harnessing himself into his large pack, and balancing the rifle on his shoulder, he seemed resigned to being seen, barely two hundred yards away. He immediately headed towards the bank of a river, flat and sandy. We realised that such a route would not be the best for him if he had wanted to be unseen as he moved along. But stubbing his bleeding feet against tree roots was no doubt becoming too painful.

We could now catch sight of him again at each loop in the river, his head shaven, his stature slight, his stride a little halting . . . Several times he looked back to check how much the distance between us was being reduced.

Towards noon, after he had taken one more look at us, I thought he was going to stop, throw down his gun and give himself up . . .

And it was then that the path he was following became impassable.

At this point the river swung round in a tight meander. As we moved beyond it we could see that the bank was swallowed up below a rock stack, a steep cliff a few dozen feet high. A stone barrier. The fugitive hesitated, went into the water, hoping to work his way round it, but came up against the obstacle again.

We slowed our pace, fearing that, with his back to the wall, he might take it into his head to fire at us, before attempting to make his escape along this wall of rock under cover of fire. In low tones, Luskas informed us of our roles in a strategy for surrounding him. ("Napoleon Bonaparte . . ." I thought, as Vassin and I exchanged brief smiles.) His manoeuvre anticipated that the enemy would remain where he was, trapped against the rocks.

"I and Major Butov will take up position here, because, if the criminal doesn't surrender, he will try to get away into the forest. Gartsev and Vassin will . . ."

But at this moment the escaped prisoner, in defiance of the logic of this plan, began clambering up the blocks of granite.

A hopeless attempt – after the first few ledges, the wall curved outwards and offered no further footholds. And worst of all, this climb left him exposed to our bullets, without him being able to return fire . . .

Disconcerted by his boldness, we had now got as far as the lower slopes of the rock face. The climber had just reached a ledge where he could only put one foot down, and Ratinsky, more febrile than ever, exclaimed: "Comrade Captain, let me finish him off." Luskas shook his head, drew his revolver and fired in the air. The escaped prisoner, poised above a drop of some fifty feet, trembled, scraped at the cliff with his other foot to find more support . . . and disappeared!

We were not close enough, where we were, down below, to have a clear view of the gap in the rock into which, slim as he was, the man had slipped, leaving only his pack visible, before completely disappearing.

"Comrade Captain, I can climb up onto . . ." Ratinsky gestured with his hand towards the cavity where the man was hiding. Cutting in ahead of Luskas, Butov answered him: "Listen, Sub-Lieutenant, that fellow will kill you as soon as you show up beneath his hiding place. Stay where you are. Let the others follow me."

Seething with resentment, Luskas flew into a rage. "I was in command of this operation from the start. I shall see it through!"

Butov looked round. "Captain, you'll be in command of it afterwards when the chain gang boss is writing his reports. Now put away that gun and come with us."

For a second I thought Luskas would not restrain himself and would shoot him in the back.

Positioning himself on the strip of ground between the riverbank and the first trees of the taiga, Butov found a location from which it was possible to see the man trying to hide in the middle of the rock terrace. Less than a hundred yards lay between us – well within effective rifle range.

Ratinsky rested his gun on a branch, ready to carry out the order to fire. Butov whistled softly, wagging his fat forefinger at him. "Save your cartridges, Sub-Lieutenant. The prisoner won't stay perched up there for long. He'll be hungry. He'll fall asleep. We'll be able to scoop him up like a fish in a landing net. Let's wait a little."

Vassin and I looked at Luskas: rapid twitches of rage and humiliation were coursing across his face. In Butov's phrase, he "shouted in a whisper": "Sub-Lieutenant, begin firing!"

Then he hissed between his teeth: "Comrade Butov, I am now in political command of this operation."

The word "political", pronounced with emphasis, had its effect: the one giving orders was no longer some vague Captain Luskas, but the representative of the regime and of its machinery of repression. To back up his words, he drew his revolver – letting it be understood that he might use it, and not only against the escaped prisoner.

Butov froze, his mouth open on a repressed oath. A living statue, he was the embodiment of the fear in which the country lived: a soldier who had risked his life during four years of war and who was now turning into a puppet, a mere "Comrade Butov", one of those whom a word from Luskas could expose to months of interrogation, to torture that could leave prisoners with their nails ripped out and their teeth broken, and to a slow death amid the ice of the Arctic Circle ...

Ratinsky's first bullet chipped the granite within inches of the fugitive's head. He hid, then reappeared and we could see that his chin was bleeding.

"I've got him!" Ratinsky cried in triumph and, in too much haste, let fly less accurately with two more bullets. The fourth caused the escaped prisoner to disappear for a much longer while, and this time I thought that it was all over with him. But he seemed to be still alive; at all events his grey shirt appeared in a gap in the rock. Ratinsky fired, the shirt vanished, as if the man had fallen, wounded more seriously, perhaps fatally.

"I think . . . that's it, Comrade Captain. The criminal's been liquidated." For more solemnity, Ratinsky stood to attention in front of Luskas. The latter had a grin of satisfaction but made a show of modesty. "Yes, the operation is finished. Let us wait a few minutes and then we'll go and bring down the body . . ."

Butov's laughter exploded with the force of a military band. He was choking, unable to speak, and waved his hand towards the cliff. Our eyes followed his gesture.

Behind a large rock, the escaped prisoner was standing upright, in such a way that his shaven head and bare shoulders could be seen. "The shirt!" Butov spat out between two bellows of laughter. "He's shafted you, Ratinsky, like he did with his hood . . . It was his shirt you made a hole in . . ."

To hide my grin from Luskas, I looked down and scratched my forehead. Vassin, too, was shaking with suppressed mirth. The trick had been the same: the escaped prisoner had taken off his shirt and hung it on the tip of a rock as a lure . . .

Suddenly Butov fell silent with a look of admiring astonishment. We raised our eyes up to the rock face once more. The escaped prisoner had not moved, but he now held a large pair of binoculars in his hands and was calmly observing us. "Non-reflective glass . . ." whispered Vassin, throwing me a wink.

Yes, they were Luskas' binoculars! Radiating hilarious satisfaction, Butov declared: "Captain, now's the moment for you to climb up and shit on a hill!"

Luskas appeared not to have heard him. He was staring at me in a way that frightened me, so dilated did each pupil appear.

His order stunned me. "Gartsev, you will climb up onto the rock!"

I stammered a refusal: "Comrade Captain. The escaped prisoner's armed and besides . . ."

He pointed the barrel of his revolver at me: "Move now!"

I edged towards the granite cliff, followed by Luskas and Vassin. The latter made an effort to keep me out of danger: "The man is surrounded, Comrade Captain. Within a couple of hours . . ."

But Luskas had calculated correctly. Having clambered up over a series of rocks we found ourselves within some fifty yards of the fugitive's place of refuge. "Go up onto that shelf!" he ordered me. I obeyed, hauling myself up a few feet higher. From there the escaped prisoner's hiding place was more easily visible. I could see that he had put his shirt on again. The top of his back appeared in the sights of my rifle.

"Fire!" Luskas' order was "shouted in a whisper", with venom directed equally at the hidden fugitive and myself.

I aimed at the granite an inch away from the shirt, swearing to myself that I would not be a murderer. There was no gun-shot in reply . . . After I had fired twice Luskas brandished his revolver. "If you miss again . . ." He had the eyes of a madman, yes, of the one who, in his sleep, used to yell, "The backs of their necks are looking at me . . ."

I made a show of taking aim with more application. The bullet ricocheted off the rock. "I'm doing my best, Comrade Captain," I heard my voice whining, so terrified that I did not recognise it. It was the voice of my "rag doll". I knew that Luskas could kill me. After so many others . . .

So the action he performed seemed logical: he stamped his foot in a violent rage. Terrified, I did not even notice that this movement coincided with a gunshot that came from the rocks.

Giving vent to a ridiculous cry of "Ow! Ooh!" he fell over. On his calf, above the top of his boot, a dark patch was spreading.

A wounded man is always a wounded man. We hastened to carry him towards the forest, to give him first aid. A tourniquet, cleansing the wound, a draught of alcohol that Butov made him drink from his flask. The bullet had passed through his calf, obviating any need for us to remove it.

Pain serves to reveal the man. Luskas showed himself to be capricious, distrustful and, in particular, lacking in stoicism. He insisted on his wound being cleansed with spirit three times. Vassin, whose kit contained the equipment and our field dressings, used up half our supply of bandages. And, for my part, I resigned myself to all the blame being heaped onto my head...

The wound would have healed quickly, but Luskas insisted that, to avoid it going septic, he needed, as a matter of urgency, to get to a place of habitation where there was a hospital. We faced a simple choice: abandon our manhunt and come home empty-handed, carrying him on a stretcher, or else set him adrift, alone, on a raft, following the course of the Amgun as far as the next village... Butov consulted the maps. A small settlement was clearly marked some ten miles downstream. All he would need to do would be to let the current carry him along.

Vassin was already busy stripping the branches off young pine trees that I cut down with his handsaw. His technique was rudimentary: a platform of tree trunks fastened together with a cord, and, on top of it, for greater stability, a second platform at right angles to the first. A pole, an oar shaped with an axe . . .

Despite all the detours the escaped prisoner had obliged us to follow through the forest, we were very close to the Amgun. Within an hour Vassin had reached it, travelling down one of the tributaries on board his craft, as we walked beside it, carrying the wounded man.

Before settling onto the raft, Luskas made us cleanse the wound again and give it a new dressing. Having killed so often, he was not unaware of the fragility of human life and clung to his own with obscene ferocity . . . He demanded one of our two rifles to take with him, "For my personal safety," he insisted, claiming that his service revolver would not be sufficient if he were attacked by wild animals. Butov observed him with contempt, muttering, "What I'd like to give him would be a grenade, with the pin removed . . ."

His leaving made its mark on us, not so much thanks to these puerile demands as to the distress evidenced by Ratinsky. He was observing the departure of the man whom he aspired to become, his dreamed-of double, his ideal. Lavishing a thousand attentions on this posturing member of the walking wounded, he spoke in tones of a mournful softness that I could never have imagined him capable of. This affection for Luskas, a being soaked in blood, made an even more striking impression on me than the joy of watching the raft as it floated away from the bank.

IV

THAT EVENING, ONCE LUSKAS HAD GONE, A REVOLUTION took place. Butov sent Ratinsky to mount guard "under the scree" at the foot of the cliff where we still believed the escaped prisoner was in hiding. The sub-lieutenant gave him a poison-ous look, but, perforce, had to obey.

The major flopped down beside the fire, and invited us – Vassin and myself – to join him. With a conjuror's ceremonious gesture, he thrust a hand into his pack and withdrew a one-litre bottle from it.

"There you are! Pure hospital spirit."

A good start had been made on the contents but Butov, noting our glances, reassured us: "This is 100 per cent. You mix one part with four parts of water . . . And don't forget that!" He crushed a handful of wild raspberries into his aluminium cup. "Better than a glass of port!"

We had some dry biscuits left, but none of the tins of the food we had been eating until then. Fortunately, in this forest where humans rarely ventured, game animals were relatively tame. For supper that evening we shared a goose Vassin had killed close to the place where the raft had been launched.

Drunkenness came quickly, garrulous and liberating, restoring what I had known during the war: the camaraderie of men who daily came within an ace of death and needed to exchange glances with their brothers in arms to feel they were still alive.

We swapped the usual soldiers' tales, stories stripped of their burden of suffering, retouched to make them shine, like medals polished up, with tooth powder, the way we used to ... Butov told of crossing the Dnieper, and painted a fine panorama of our armies in action, untouched by shelling from the Germans. I told them about a Baltic town where the regiment I was embedded with as a war correspondent had come upon a cellar overflowing with fine wines. Vassin, who was less forthcoming, alluded to the defence of Leningrad ...

As dusk fell, the wind brought down a drizzle with an already autumnal chill. We took refuge in one of the tents and tried to resume our banquet with the same convivial mood as before. But the alcohol – that inevitable one draught too many – now brought on bitterness, a sad lucidity, with admissions we could no longer thrust into the background.

"Yes, we did cross the Dnieper," sighed Butov. "It's just that ... There were so many killed that to secure the pontoons, the engineers were driving their pillars into a layer of corpses ..."

I recalled the alleyway where the women lay who had been shot by the Germans, and I was just about to mention it, when Butov suddenly stuck his head out of the tent and shouted in the direction of the rock face: "Hey, Ratinsky! Come and have a drink!" Meanwhile in Vassin's half-closed eyes I sensed a memory of the war that had little in common with our boastful yarns.

Ratinsky quickly became drunk and, to match our stories, declared emphatically, "I was too young to join up . . . But I lived in the occupied zone on the Polish frontier and I did my bit against the Nazis!"

There followed a list of exploits: a road sign turned to point the other way, the tyres of a military vehicle punctured . . . As he gathered momentum, he would doubtless have invented an even more glorious past for himself, claiming a role in the Resistance, but the alcohol muddled him as he was getting into his stride . . . Flying off at a tangent, he began talking about his grandfather, a "senior official in the Empire of the tsars", an "aristocrat" who governed a province in his native Poland – Russian at the time – "with an iron fist". And also about his father, who had received an inheritance from the aforementioned iron fist, but had offered his services to the Soviets . . . Ratinsky repeated the word "iron" in almost every sentence. Clearly order and military rule fascinated him, and, as I listened to him, I gained a better understanding of the admiration with which he regarded Luskas.

Waxing more fiery, he downed another draught, barely diluted, and snorted like a horse galloping ashore: "Phew! Oh yes! . . . An iron discipline! From my childhood my father gave me the taste for it – everything in its place, every man in his station. I used to watch the Germans during the war, there was a military headquarters in the town where I lived. Well, with them it's clear: order is order. In a German officer, you can feel it, in his movements, in his voice. With us it's all a shambles, anarchy, and then, before you know where you are, it's a dictatorship and heads roll! When the Germans move into a town the cars are gleaming, the uniforms are impeccable and, above all, when you're working for them, no surprises! You're paid well for what you do ... Ah ... Well, no! I'm not talking about myself! What I mean is, in principle ..."

He became confused and, with an insight that pierced through his drink-befuddled mind, it must have dawned on him that he had given himself away appallingly. He had a choking fit. He spluttered, spitting out pieces of meat ... Butov eyed us, Vassin and myself, as if to ask: "What can be done about this fellow?" Then, with an expression more sympathetic than severe, he thumped Ratinsky on the back a few times, for he was coughing enough to rip his lungs out.

When his fit had subsided, Butov sighed. "Listen, Sub-Lieutenant . . . you're lucky that Luskas isn't here. He'd have put you behind bars for a quarter of what you've just told us ... Go and sober up! Gartsev will mount guard in your place ..."

Ratinsky stood up and tried to speak but all he could manage was a plaintive hiccup. When he had gone, Butov remarked softly: "That's always the way in life ... You come to someone's rescue and you end up wondering what vile trick he'll play on you by way of thanks ... Very well, we'll see. Tomorrow, no rush. We'll have our grub peacefully and move on, taking our time. That's fine. Our Napoleon Bonaparte's gone. As for the escaped prisoner, I'm sure he'll wait for us. It's not in his interests to see a whole new search party come rushing out.

So, let's make the best of our time on leave here. Who knows what awaits us on our return . . ."

He alluded to this "return" in bitter, astonishingly sober tones.

At my post beneath the cliff face I reflected that, after Ratinsky's involuntary admissions, I loathed him less. Yes, of course he was a filthy, self-seeking sneak. And his work for the Germans! But . . . I pictured him as a child, a little offshoot of Polish nobility, all at sea in an era soaked in blood by revolutions and civil wars. In order to survive he had found a lifebelt: the "iron discipline" that he admired in his father, in the Germans, in Luskas. Without this he would never have broken free from that adolescent hiding within him – a sickly boy, afraid lest people remind him of his grandfather's tsarist past and his family's dubious origins in that pre-war Poland that had got into bed with Hitler. And above all, his juvenile admiration for smart Nazi officers . . . Every one of those flaws could cost him long years in a prison camp.

A hidden adolescent. Pretty similar, all things considered, to that "rag doll" I carried within myself. That frenzied symbol of our will to survive, to love, to win recognition, to be loved . . .

For the first time I experienced this feeling of the roles being interchangeable: Butov, Vassin and . . . yes, even Ratinsky. And also that fugitive, huddled up there amid the rocks. A poor wretch with bloodied feet, who must be beginning to perceive us as individuals, each with his inner "rag doll", and all yoked together in this absurd chase . . .

When he came to relieve me, Vassin settled down beside the fire and quietly remarked with a vaguely sheepish air: "I didn't want to talk about the fighting around Leningrad earlier on . . . The truth is that our unit was protecting the civilians who were being evacuated in lorries driven across the lake on the ice. One night I watched a truck, carrying about fifty children, disappearing through a hole opened up by a bomb. By the next day the ice had frozen over and the vehicles went on shuttling back and forth, as before. Since then, I've lost a taste for these soldiers' tales. People embellish them. They're all about heroic deeds and victories. The younger generation listens and then starts dreaming about wars of its own . . ."

I hesitated for a moment, then admitted: "There wasn't a cellar full of wine in that Baltic town I was talking about. Just a crate of bottles I drank up with the squaddies, so as to forget that we'd been trampling over the faces of dead people. Since then I've never found any other way of forgetting . . ."

ON THE MORNING AFTER OUR BANQUET WE ESTABLISHED that the escaped prisoner had made the effort to scale the rock barrier and continue on his way. We were secretly relieved by this: no final confrontation and a few more days "on leave", as Butov had put it.

Our life combined the elements of an existence that any man could have envied us. We were walking beside streams that flowed through untouched forests, we would halt in places that mirrored the stops made by the fugitive, we ate game grilled over the fire, and at night, over dinners laced with drink, we had thoroughly manly conversations: war, women, hunting, guns . . .

The person we were pursuing had become essential to this simple happiness! Even Ratinsky was carried away by it. One afternoon he bathed in a shallow little lake warmed by the sun – a puny body, with prominent shoulder blades best kept hidden beneath a uniform . . .

The escaped prisoner seemed to divine our mood of enjoying an interlude. At night his three fires burned ever closer to where we were – he judged an attack by us to be unlikely.

"He'll end up collapsing with exhaustion, you'll see," Butov would remark. "In fact, it puzzles me how he can still be on his feet" . . . And we sensed that he hoped to see this walker survive several more stages in the journey before he gave way.

One evening we were dining off taimen, a fish of some 20 pounds that Vassin had speared. Suddenly, in the triangle of fires that marked out the fugitive's camp, his shadowy figure could be made out! Two hundred yards away, at most, from our own camping ground. Butov, already very tipsy, rose to his feet. Using his hands as a megaphone, he yelled: "Comrade! Don't stay there on your own. Come and have a drink with us!" In spite of our roars of laughter, his shouted words left us feeling oddly sad. Butov was about to propose a toast, doubtless as playful as his invitation addressed to the escaped prisoner. But his voice faded away into a growled remark: "He may well have been slandered, that fellow. Just one denunciation and quick as a flash he's an 'enemy of the people'! He doesn't have the look of a murderer. Otherwise he'd have shot us all last night, drunk as we were . . ."

I watched Ratinsky, certain that he would be reporting these subversive remarks. However, he remained detached, nodding pensively at Butov's words.

That night – as I would later understand – we came as close as we ever would to what was the best in us.

Thanks to the blissful absent-mindedness of our progress, dates are mixed up in my memory. Two days passed, or perhaps even three, in this state of carefree forgetfulness.

Then the shock of a stunning discovery upset this tranquil mood.

We woke before sunrise – with no plans for an attack on the escaped prisoner, but feeling the chill of the first frost. As yet, nothing in the foliage around us betrayed the arrival of autumn, but the breeze from the Sea of Okhotsk was already depositing hoar frost crystals on the canvas of our tents.

This sent a signal that must have made Butov uneasy, giving him visions of the taiga invaded by snowdrifts, the pathways erased, landmarks invisible. Morosely he announced: "Right, the holidays are over. Today we're going to catch him, this fellow. It's time to go home." This decision may also have been due to his hangover and the exhaustion of his reserves of alcohol.

We breakfasted quickly and set off, in accordance with his plan of attack: to surround the escaped prisoner's camp and harry him, by firing close to his feet …

Our noose drew tighter: in the morning mist we saw that the man, caught off guard, was trying to slip into a thicket. As we fired shots all around him, he was struggling amid the branches. We went right up to the place he had retreated to, Butov and Ratinsky aiming with their revolvers, me gripping the only rifle left to us, Vassin holding a strap to bind him with …

We rushed into the thicket with shouts of: "Hands up! Don't move or I'll fire!"

He wasn't there … Searching through the clump of bushes this way and that we finally came upon a long cord attached to a shrub. So that was his trick: he tugged on the line, the branches shook, attracting us towards this hiding place, while he, concealed behind a tree, prepared to make his escape.

But our operation had not been fruitless. The fugitive had only just got away, abandoning his pack, some smoked fish, a beaker fashioned from birch bark and several faded pieces of fabric that were drying over the embers – bandages for his wounds, no doubt.

One of these strips of cotton, which he had evidently just removed, bore traces of blood. Ratinsky crowed: "I was the one that hit him where it hurts, that fellow! Look, he's still bleeding. Yes, it was me . . ."

Butov examined the cotton with its brown stain, and then, wide-eyed, gasped with an incredulity in which rage was mingled with admiration: "She's shafted the lot of us, the bitch!"

With a gesture of disgust he flung the cloth into the embers, turned to Ratinsky and muttered through gritted teeth: "If you want to hit this one where it hurts, you'll need your prick. You'd do better to stop bragging and take a look at this. It's her time of the month, you idiot."

Everything that had seemed odd to us now became clear: the escaped prisoner's modest stature, her footprints being much smaller than ours, her face, her gait . . .

In a fury, Butov gave his orders: "The same plan of attack. We surround her, we fire at her feet, we corner her . . . And then we're going to hammer her, all four of us, the filthy cow!"

To us the violence of his tone seemed fully justified. The fact that the escaped prisoner had turned out to be a woman had radically changed our attitude. Before, we had had a vague sympathy for this barefoot fugitive. He was the embodiment of what could happen to any one of us in the appalling and unpredictable era that we lived in.

To be confronted by a woman turned the whole sense of our expedition upside down. She had humiliated and belittled us. Now we were the real victims. Endlessly shunted this way and that in this interminable taiga. Our honour under attack. Cut down to size by a girl who was a better shot than any of us, who kept going at a spirited pace, responded coolly to every assault. And worst of all, though capable of killing us, she had avoided being a bringer of death!

I was turning all these notions over in my mind, to get a grip on the staggering novelty of the situation. And then I did so again, so as to temper the fever of desire: this woman's body I was to enjoy along with the others, a bitch who must be punished, not for her crime but for having perverted the logic of this world!

"The thing is," Ratinsky was holding forth as we halted, "if a woman goes to prison, that means she's a thief, or else she's a bad mother. Or even worse: maybe she's killed her husband. There are lots of those in the camps . . . I know a thing or two about that!"

It took no great effort on my part to justify the coital feast that lay ahead. In one corner of my mind the fugitive was associated with Sveta and inspired the same mixture of jealousy and resentment.

123

We stepped up our pace and when we reached tight meanders in the river we found we were now coming so close to the woman that our eyes could make out the movement of her hips beneath the coarse fabric of her clothes, the slender line of her neck . . . Only her weapon, carried upside down on her shoulder, checked our urge to run up to her, push her over and crush her into the sand. Now, more than ever, firing at her was out of the question – her body must remain intact for our satisfaction.

Ratinsky, the youngest among us, could hardly wait. Several times I noticed him distractedly fingering the crotch of his trousers. At a ford where the distance between us and the fugitive had shrunk to less than fifty yards, he whispered with enraged insistence: "Major, I'm going in. I'll catch her as she's crossing. I know I can do it . . ."

Butov, his face red from the excitement of the chase, uttered an indistinct grunt, signalling tacit approval, his eyes riveted to the figure of the woman whose wet garments brazenly emphasised the curve and movement of her buttocks as she waded on . . .

Ratinsky moved forward with great strides, stumbling on rocks, slipping on slabs of clay made invisible by the speed of the current. He had managed to cover half the distance when the woman appeared to be missing her footing and falling. She thrust one arm into the water, seeking to support herself on the bottom, her other arm holding up the rifle to keep it above the surface. Ratinsky rushed towards his helpless prey . . .

Then the fugitive stood upright and we thought that she

was about to playfully splash her pursuer. No, it was a small stone that she threw at him with astonishing precision. Hit on the head, Ratinsky spun round, as if to call on us as witnesses. In reality, it was the violence of the impact that sent him into this half turn. He tottered and sat down in the middle of the ford with the water up to his neck, looking for all the world like a child vexed at being refused a sweetie.

For a fraction of a second the rest of us had just seen the woman's face. Slanting eyes with prominent cheekbones, like those of all the native peoples of the far eastern territories. Her hair, which was starting to grow back on her shaven head, was of a charcoal grey like that of the locals. A "Tungus" ... For us, this generic term was evocative of backward populations lost in impenetrable forests in the prehistoric time of the shamans. That was no doubt why we felt no shame in contemplating rape – this woman belonged to a world of wild nature, like a partridge, whose neck one wrings without much compunction ...

We caught up with Ratinsky, our "serious casualty" and helped him to pick himself up. "Don't worry, Sub-Lieutenant," Butov consoled him. "You shall be the first to screw her. It's like fishing – the more the pike fights back, the better the sport ..."

Once we had reached the far bank, we continued our pursuit, but the sun was already low; it was time to light a fire against another frost ...

JUST BEFORE NOON THE FOLLOWING DAY, AT THE MOMENT of our halt, we noticed smoke rising towards the sun from behind a screen of willows. "There she is!" whispered Ratinsky and, without any of us being allotted roles, we broke into a run. Aflame with desire, Butov even forgot he still had his aluminium mug in his hand. The same vision spurred us all on: that of the "Tungus woman" supine on the ground, with spread thighs and bare breasts.

We found ourselves on the bank of a river where the current was not as fast as that of the tributaries we normally crossed. Separated from us by some twenty yards, the fugitive was on the opposite shore, standing in the water up to her hips ...

She was completely naked! Her body had the muscular slimness of a hardened walker, a torso sculpted by physical effort, breasts firm and round. The glow from her skin gilded by the sun hurt our eyes ... After a moment of bemusement we rushed into the water.

The woman did not seem alarmed. She splashed her face, turned round and strolled back up towards her fire. Just the sight of her walking drove us mad ...

Ratinsky, who was several steps ahead of us, plunged in first, then it was the turn of Butov and myself. Vassin, more prudently, remained on the bank, gripping our rifle in his hands.

The bottom of this sluggish watercourse, on the side where we had waded in, was deep in mud. Immersed to above our knees in a deposit of silt, we found ourselves struggling amid a murky mixture from which bubbles that stank of decay rose gurgling to the surface . . . Ratinsky, almost tragic with his red lump on his brow, ended up shouting out: "Help! I'm drowning in this filth!" I held out my hand to Butov, who, forming a rescue chain, grabbed the sub-lieutenant . . .

We scrambled back onto the bank. The fugitive, barely hidden by a willow tree, was drying herself beside the fire. Butov, overcome by a bull-like fury, yelled: "We'll get you, you slag! Tomorrow we'll all go through you! Every orifice!"

The woman's reaction was unexpected. She picked up the rifle that lay on the ground beside her, aimed at Butov and fired.

Instinctively we all rushed over to him, afraid we should have to pick up a corpse. But the major remained upright. Speechless, his eyes popping out of his head, he showed us the mug he still held in his hand. The metal had been pierced, in one side and out the other, with two neat holes.

That evening we compensated for it with talk.

Butov drew up a list of "all the bitches" he had "had it off with" during his life. Among them, the conquest he was most proud of was a minister's wife! We thought her status was probably exaggerated, but a good storyline justified such minor modifications. The wife in question used to pounce on the young Butov like a tigress. "One day we were going at it hammer and tongs and all of a sudden her husband, the minister, shows up. There's a big saloon car under the windows and his driver's opening the door for him . . . The woman panics. 'He'll throw you in prison!' Quick as a flash, I hide my uniform, grab some trousers and a pullover from a wardrobe, put them on in two seconds flat and lie down on the bathroom floor with my head under the bath. The woman caught on. The husband comes in. She kisses him. 'Darling, we've got a leaking pipe! But luckily I've found a plumber!' He'd just come in to change for an official dinner . . ."

We exploded with exaggerated laughter, and drank toasts to the gallantry of soldiers versus bureaucrats. Butov stopped up the holes in his mug with his thumb and forefinger as he drank . . .

I told them the story of my amorous setback. Sveta became a grasping young beauty who scorned a valiant warrior (me), preferring a field marshal's son who'd spent his time polishing the seat of his trousers at staff headquarters. My narrative elicited a surge of sincere sympathy. Butov punctuated my words with resounding cries of: "Oh no, what a bitch!" Ratinsky curled his mouth into a rhetorical grimace of disgust: "So who wants to love them, these tarts, after that? . . ."

From time to time Vassin uttered a sympathetic sigh. My tale ended with a pitched battle: I punched the daddy's boy, turned to the treacherous woman and flung all the money I had on me in her face . . . Butov was so enthusiastic about this denouement that he forgot to block the holes in his mug, and lost a good draught of alcohol.

Ratinsky, for his part, again went too far. "Before joining the army I served as a guard in a camp," he proclaimed and, despite our drunkenness, we felt an icy chill run up our spines. "No, not here. We were up in the north, at Vorkuta. And I should tell you that, as regards having it away, there wasn't much to celebrate. But he who seeks, finds. As soon as a new batch arrived at the women's camp next door, we went in, chose a girl and made it clear to her: 'Right, either you agree to sleep with us or we'll make you work so hard it'll kill you.' They quickly became accommodating ... Only one refused. Beautiful, young. Sentenced for anti-Soviet propaganda. We tried everything: solitary confinement, inhuman labour, threats, everything. She didn't yield. So then we took her out into the forest and screwed her fit to make a sieve of her. There were ten of us, we weren't joking. We even broke her arm ... And when it was over, we said to her: 'And now piss off. Get lost!' She took a few steps and we shot her and the case was recorded as 'attempted escape'. That's what we should do tomorrow with that bitch who's leading us a dance in this bloody taiga!"

He grabbed his mug, drank, screwing up his eyes and belched ... His recital sobered us. Stunned, we watched his Adam's apple sliding up and down as he swallowed, sitting there with his thin legs comically crossed. Butov's jaws moved silently, he was at a loss for how to express a jumble of emotions: contempt and aversion, but also shame that, such a little time earlier, he had had the urge to rape a woman, just like in Ratinsky's story.

Through his drunkenness, the sub-lieutenant must have sensed the meaning of that long look directed at him. He pressed his hands against the ground, rose to his feet, performed the semblance of a military salute and walked over to his tent.

The wind was dispersing the fumes of alcohol, bringing us close to the extreme clear-headedness one rarely reaches without first having drunk. Butov, ill at ease, took out the bottle and upended it over his mug, but could only elicit a few drops from it . . . He pulled a face and attempted a joke ("Well, that's torn it. I run on firewater. If there's none left, I'm going home . . ."). But he broke off and began speaking again in quite different tones. Sorrowful and earnest. "That girl we can't manage to catch, she, too, may have had someone who loved her. Who can say? I met my wife during the war. A nurse. All around there were bombs, filth, blood. I had a bellyful of shell splinters. I was dying, the doctor didn't hide it from me . . . Suddenly there was this little white coat! I looked up at it and said to myself, 'This must be like being in heaven. You see a face, you're happy, and that's all you need . . .' And then I got better and . . . Once more I needed a lot of things. Money, rank, food, women. I married the nurse . . . After the war she took her revenge on hunger, she put on weight. She even became a handsome woman, a real officer's wife, if you know what I mean. Commanding, fierce, a bit of a sergeant major in a skirt. And that other woman, the one I'd seen when I was dying, she no longer existed . . . The priests are always telling us, you know, how man is punished for his sins. In other words, damnation and hellfire. But the real punishment isn't that . . . It's when the woman you've loved disappears . . . how can I put it? Yes, she disappears inside the one who goes on living with you . . ."

He seemed not to have fully grasped the truth of what he had just been saying. Hearing the crackle of a brand in the fire, he roused himself. "Right . . . Gartsev, you stay on guard for a bit, just in case . . . Vassin or I will relieve you in three hours . . . Well I never! Look, she doesn't even hide anymore . . ."

In the darkness the silhouette of the fugitive was outlined against her three fires – calm movements, a soothing sequence of actions preparatory to sleep.

As I kept watch my thoughts came up against the puzzling simplicity of our lives. There was this woman, in her solitary night, and here, so very close to her, ourselves – men who, a few hours earlier, were ready to submit her to the torture of a bestial assault . . . Philosophers used to claim that man was corrupted by society and bad rulers. And yet all that the blackest regime could have done, at worst, was to order us to kill this fugitive. Not to inflict on her the torment of multiple rape. No, the rapist dwelled within ourselves, like a virus, and no ideal society could have cured us. In me, it was that "rag doll", the guardian of my lust for life. In Ratinsky, the little Polish adolescent quaking at the thought of missing out on success and pleasure. In Butov . . . What doppelgänger inhabited the vast body that had gorged itself on female flesh? And Vassin, who preferred to keep quiet, but who, he too, had rushed up to the riverbank following the pack of us?

Thanks to the rag doll embedded in all our brains, any idea of improving humanity was a chimera. The great doctors of the soul hoped to eliminate the bacillus that impelled us to hate, lie and kill. But, without it, the world would have had no history, no wars, no great men.

I thought about Ratinsky's story: a woman violated by camp guards and shot on the pretext of an escape – always the need to exonerate oneself vis-à-vis the social order! The banal monstrosity of this murder had brought us to our senses for a time, laying bare our own vileness. So maybe that was the solution: the image of a corpse as a spoiler to sexual fantasy . . .

The fugitive's fires were glowing feebly in the darkness. I recalled the day when I had caught sight of her prisoner's smock in the middle of an interrupted darning session. At the time I had been terrified that the escaped prisoner, cornered as he was, was going to shoot me . . . I now recalled those moments completely differently. The light shining on the fabric, the wind ruffling the tops of the pine trees and the words I should have spoken: "Don't be afraid. I'm walking away. I won't harm you. I shan't tell anyone you're there . . ."

Such a reverie seemed quite improbable now; with a sigh, I pulled an anguished face. Then suddenly I realised that everything had, in effect, happened on that day precisely as it had in my fantasy: I had encountered Luskas and I had concealed the presence of the escaped prisoner from him. And for several minutes I could no longer feel any "rag doll" within myself!

Vassin appeared, carrying an armful of branches, revived the fire and said to me: "Go and get some sleep, Pavel. Tomorrow

Butov really wants to bring our games of hare and hounds to an end. He told me to wake everyone at five ..."

Still too distant from the reality of our lives, I clumsily attempted to match the tone of our earlier conversations.

"Bring to an end is easily said ... We'll have a job. Especially if Butov gives a repeat performance of his rutting bull act. And, as for Ratinsky, he may well have been pissed, but his story was clear. He wouldn't hesitate to rape the girl and then liquidate her, as he's done before ..."

I was expecting Vassin to agree with what I had said, which, all things considered, was beyond dispute. But he retorted, emphasising every word: "I don't for one moment believe he's taken part in rape and murder. He must just have heard people talking about it and felt jealous of the bastards who did it. And that's almost worse than murder itself."

This judgment seemed to me too out of hand, as if Vassin were trying to set himself apart from us. Without concealing my irritation, I replied: "Alright . . . Butov and he lost their heads, but you can see why. This Tungus woman's a hell of a little siren . . . Me too, I'd not have said no. Even you, Mark, admit it, she took your fancy as well. Otherwise you'd not have come running along with the rest of us like a lad of sixteen. And what's more, I noticed you brought the gun with you! That was so you could threaten the girl, wasn't it?"

The flames blazed up, caught by the wind, and Vassin turned away to avoid the smoke, blinking.

His voice became more muted. "I took the gun because the first one of you who'd gone for that girl, I'd have shot him dead."

THE FOLLOWING MORNING WE GOT OFF TO A START IN BEST military fashion. Reveille before dawn, on the move with no words exchanged, orders given with a thrust of the chin. No action plan needed now, each of us knew his role. Our "holidays" were over, all we had to do now was to arrest the woman and escort her back to the camp.

The imminence of this return gave me an uneasy feeling, that of having found myself in front of a house hidden deep in the forest, poised on the brink of thrusting open the gate that led to it, then turning away and going back to my old life. The others, too, must have seen this end to our wanderings as the vanishing of an opportunity to cross a threshold into the unknown . . .

We advanced the way we used to when Luskas was dragooning us into night operations: darkness, tension, the fugitive's fires and, given away by the glow from them, a body (her body?) lying there fast asleep.

And this further coincidence, a tree trunk lying across a river. In conspiratorial whispers we concluded that this bridge was undoubtedly a trap! Should we look for a ford, at the risk of alerting the girl? Between the three glowing sets of embers the outstretched body stirred, curled up and was still again. "We'll go this way," whispered Butov. "Wait here. I'll check everything. This time she won't trick us ..."

He moved forward, took one step onto the tree trunk and jumped up and down on it to check any instability. But the timber remained firm and the river was neither as wide nor as fast flowing as the one that had swallowed up our rifles.

Butov was halfway across when, as in the repetition of a bad dream, his foot slipped and struck against the tree trunk, throwing his hefty body off balance. He uttered an oath and this was followed by the sound of him falling plump into the water.

By the pale light of dawn we were able to see him clinging to a huge rock close to the far shore. Vassin and I forded the stream lower down. Ratinsky, who did not want to get his clothes wet, used the bridge, slipped as well, but managed to cling on to the tree trunk and avoid taking a dip.

The icy water anaesthetised the pain and Butov was not at first aware of the seriousness of the sprain. He was even able to reach us and detect the trap: the fallen tree had been smeared with grease from a fish – we found the remains of a taimen in the grass.

Most amazing of all was the calm with which the fugitive left the scene. We saw her gathering up her things, stamping on the embers and moving on. Butov, still winded from his fall, tried to chase after her, suddenly gave a yell and collapsed. I had difficulty in removing his left boot – his ankle was swelling visibly ...

*

We spent the day preparing for his departure. In view of the passenger's weight, Vassin was obliged to construct a raft of "superior tonnage", as he put it with a smile. Unlike Luskas, Butov was uncomplaining and even proposed to leave his revolver with us. We refused: "Bears, wolves, you never know . . ." As the craft floated away, he called out, by way of farewell: "You ought to be coming with me! You'll never catch that girl. She must be ten hours away from here by now."

As the raft disappeared into the distance, I was left with the sense of an end to those days of freedom. And also a regret, vain now, at not having thrust open a gate into the unknown.

Butov was wrong. That evening, when we went back to that fallen tree trunk, we saw the smoke arising from a camp. Vassin summed up the situation. "We're her bodyguard. As long as our intrepid team is on the case, they're not going to send in fellows cleverer than us. She knows that . . ."

At these words Ratinsky thrust out his chin and declared: "Her games of hide and seek are over. Tomorrow we'll get her cornered. I'm in command of operations now."

Vassin and I exchanged perplexed glances. Thanks to Butov, we had stopped taking things too seriously.

No, Ratinsky was not joking. The following day we advanced without stopping, we ate on foot and, after crossing a river, we no longer took the time to dry off. The woman was beginning to lose the lead she had on us. On several occasions Vassin showed me footprints marked with blood.

It was clear that Ratinsky took himself for Luskas, and on the evening of that gruelling day he had a particularly absurd idea. To "destabilise" the fugitive, he ordered us to spend the night repeatedly moving from one position to another, each time lighting a fire, which would give her the impression of an ever tighter encirclement. He himself would remain "at the command post", which was how he pompously designated Luskas and Butov's tent.

Unconvinced, we carried out our nocturnal migration from one fire to another. The taiga, its slumber disturbed, hurled mud flats beneath our feet, into which we were plunged up to our knees, and constantly blocked our path as we fumbled our way blindly through thickets . . .

At about three o'clock in the morning we climbed up onto a hill and could see several of our fires. Unevenly spaced, they were dotted around the triangle of glowing embers at whose centre, we believed, lay the fugitive's camp. Vassin sat down, holding his hands out towards the flames of our latest fire. "I'm not going any further. Ratinsky can go to the devil with all these japes and tricks!"

I agreed with him. "And this marathon of his is unlikely to work. Luskas kept driving us on all the time, you remember, but the girl was always too quick for us . . ."

Vassin made no reply and I thought he had just fallen asleep. "She wasn't always that quick," he murmured eventually. "Luskas managed to corner her more than once. Remember the day she was trapped up on that cliff. It would have been easy to catch her . . . But you were the one, Pavel, who chose not to aim straight."

I wasn't clear whether this was a simple observation of fact or a reproach. I gave an evasive answer: "Luskas was tickling my ribs with his revolver. It was hard for me to perform like a crack marksman ..."

Vassin's eye glinted in the firelight. "No, you did it on purpose, Pavel. You wanted to save her. And I know why ..."

His mysterious air made me uneasy, and I replied in rather mocking tones: "Oh, come off it, Mark. You were ready to bump us all off to protect that girl when she was skinny-dipping ..."

I sensed that my casual manner had struck a false note. Vassin lowered his eyes and subsided physically, as if all his bone structure had suddenly been removed. I thought about his age, markedly greater than mine, but this shrinking into himself had nothing to do with those extra years of his.

"It's because the fugitive looks very much like ... like my wife," he said in a soft voice.

I did not have the wit to abandon my glib tones. "But that girl must be years younger than your wife. Unless you're married to a student ..."

He replied with bitter simplicity and no resentment at my banter. "No, the fugitive must be about the same age. Yes, the age my wife was when she died. It was during the war. I told you about it. The siege of Leningrad, when they were evacuating civilians by the route across ice on Lake Ladoga. My wife was in a lorry, one of the ones that sank through holes opened up by the bombing. With the children from her school ... and our son. He was seven. After the war I asked the city administration if there was any possibility of retrieving the bodies. The official

I met was yawning as he listened to me. Then he cut in: 'For burial? We've got a million corpses stashed away all over the place, without coffins or tombstones, and you're talking about the ones in the lake? The fish can take care of them . . .' I hit him and broke his nose. They arrested me. I got seven years in Vorkuta, that place where Ratinsky told us he'd served."

Vassin fell silent. Contrite, I tried to make up for my clumsiness.

"And you didn't try to explain to the judges the reason for your anger? There were extenuating circumstances they should have considered!"

"I didn't give it any more thought. In fact, by then I barely existed anymore. Not in this world, at least. I told myself that if people could go on living in spite of that lorry at the bottom of a frozen lake, then this world wasn't worth very much. In the camp I met a priest, a prisoner like me. He talked to me about how God loves us. About the light in the depths of the abyss . . . He was sticking to his script. I didn't reply. There was no point. You see, both before and after the deaths of those children, people have never stopped killing and burning and . . . yawning! The apparatchik who saw me was being more honest than the priest. At least he wasn't banging on about the light of God . . ."

He broke off, nodding gently at his own thoughts. Then, stretching out his arm towards the forest, he whispered: "Look, Pavel! There it is! The divine light in the darkness. Our fires, lit to deceive that woman. Yes, trickery, lies, brute force, conquest. Human life. A little kid would be amazed: what's it all for? Here, in this lovely taiga beneath this star-studded sky. But adults are not amazed. They find explanations: war, enemies of the people . . . And then, when it all becomes too much, they talk about God, about hope! Those children drowned beneath the ice. What good is that divine light to them?"

His voice came close to a suppressed sob. I hastened to ask a question. "But you didn't serve your full sentence, did you?"

He gave a wry smile. "Four years later the bureaucrat who yawned when he was listening to me was accused of Trotsky-ism. They began checking on all the people he'd had dealings with . . . After four years in the camp they brought me out of my hut for questioning. I told them what had passed between him and me. So now I had become the innocent victim of an appalling conspirator . . . No, the judge wasn't acting out of compassion. He just needed to give a boost to his own file. So I was rehabilitated, without knowing that one day I should find myself hunting down an escaped prisoner . . ."

One of the fugitive's fires blazed up with a livelier glow. In the darkness we could not tell if she was poking it or if, as often happens, the flames were flaring up as a prelude to dying down.

Vassin seemed to hesitate before sharing with me what was in his mind. "When they released me I realised the simplest thing would be to kill myself. I didn't do it, because I still some-times had dreams in which I saw my wife and our boy. I wasn't too sure of having the same chance once I was dead."

He spoke, as if to himself: "When I first caught sight of the fugitive – I realised she was a woman on the fourth night of our hunt – all I wanted to do was to follow in her footsteps day after day and, by night, to watch her fires. This would have been enough to convince me that the light of God does exist. No, no, not that light, that's too much! Just to believe that something other than our own lives exists. Another life. One in which I could be following in this woman's footsteps without ever catching up with her . . . But I suppose that sounds rather like a fairy tale doesn't it?"

He gave a sigh and picked up our rifle, which was lying on the ground, remarking softly: "I know you're not going to fire at her, but can I tell you that, in any case, I've offset the sights. At a hundred yards, the bullet will deviate to the right by the breadth of a man's head."

RATINSKY'S TACTIC ("KEEP WALKING TILL YOU DROP" WAS how Vassin described it) produced the expected result: the fugitive was almost constantly within sight. Weakened by this relentless pursuit, she mistook her way, retraced her steps and, not even stopping to drink, collected water in the hollow of her hand. One night she did not light a fire, something that had never happened before. "She's lying low now, like a she-wolf that's had its feet broken," sneered Ratinsky.

I remembered Vassin's words: to spend a lifetime walking ever onwards, with one's eyes fixed on the distant figure of this woman. A fairy tale . . .

The next day she crossed a river, no doubt hoping to be hidden in the undergrowth on the opposite bank. But this bank turned out to be just a narrow island. She made her way along it, at times finding herself only a few dozen yards away from us. A cornered she-wolf (Ratinsky was right about that) would have bared her teeth. The fugitive, for her part, took aim with her rifle two or three times to instil respect in us. At length, seeing no way out, she moved towards the spot where the river formed rapids.

Granite boulders, some of them washed over by cascades of water, others protruding out of whirlpools, offered no safe route across. You had to be desperate to attempt to get over there. The fugitive climbed up onto a chain of rocks, hesitated, leaned on her rifle, as if on a stick, went down into the water up to her chest, and climbed up onto another rock, struggling against the torrent.

"Go after her, Vassin," shouted Ratinsky. "Make her fall. Gartsev, you go into the water further downstream, so she can't escape by swimming. Move now!"

Vassin objected: "Comrade Sub-Lieutenant, she won't be able to make it across. The current's too strong. She's got halfway with no rock to give her a foothold. She's bound to come back to us."

Already confident of his success, Ratinsky yelled: "I'm in command here! I tell you, go after her. Quickly!" Deliberately or not, he slapped the holster of his revolver.

Vassin took off his pack, looked at me as if asking for help, then followed hard on the fugitive's heels.

The woman was approaching the middle of the river, the gap between the rocks where the water came hurtling through unimpeded at a furious rate. Stationed downstream in water that froze my diaphragm, I was watching her hazardous balancing act with bated breath.

She paused, irresolute. The nearest boulder was more than a yard ahead of her. She would therefore need to jump from a standing start and, above all, manage to cling onto the surface of the rock, which was rounded and green with moss. She assessed the danger at a glance, looked back and saw Vassin, who was painfully advancing from one stepping stone to the next, as well as me, barring a possible escape down the stream. On the bank Ratinsky was aiming his revolver at her, to emphasise his role as commander of the operation.

The woman's next action left me dumbfounded. She drew out a blade attached to her belt – I could see it was a bayonet – and fitted it onto her rifle. The manoeuvre seemed absurd: she was surely not going to charge at Vassin! Furthermore this made the rifle even longer and more cumbersome.

I had no time to think of an explanation. She crouched down and, flexing her legs, launched herself into the channel where the water came swirling through. Certain of seeing her carried away by the current, I moved forward so as to be able to catch her . . . But in the midst of all the turbulence she seemed to be resisting the force of the stream between the rock she had just jumped down from and the one she needed to get to. As she moved towards this latter mass of stone, all became clear: the rifle, lengthened by the bayonet, was forming a bar, a link between the two granite surfaces, and supporting her as she crossed . . .

Ratinsky, who had just grasped this, uttered a hysterical yell, urging Vassin to move forward faster. This shout had the opposite effect: Vassin stumbled, slipped, lost his balance, fell over backwards and was swept down towards the foaming waters at the brink of the next rapid.

In the end, he was the one I was obliged to haul out. If his head had caught against the edge of a rock, he could have drowned.

Regaining his composure, he asked me to help him take his boots off. He also removed his trousers: there was a large gash on his right knee. He took hold of it, felt it and in muted tones noted: "That's it. I've just smashed a kneecap . . . So ends the fairy tale."

The rest of the day was spent in making a raft. I sawed the tree trunks and fastened them together, following Vassin's instructions. Ratinsky harried us with reproaches, but did not seem too anxious: the fugitive had barely had the strength to cross the river and collapse on the far side. Just beyond a willow grove we could see the fire she had lit to dry her clothes. Her decision to stay where she was, so close to us, was no longer a ploy. She must be incapable of setting off again on her lacerated feet.

Meanwhile Ratinsky had discovered a ford. Like a bolt from the blue, he informed me of his assault plan. Early the next morning, once Vassin had been sent on his way, we would "arrest the criminal in the proper manner". He seemed to have swallowed his anger, confident that he alone was now the true conqueror.

That night, as I kept watch, I was fashioning a splint for Vassin: rods bound together by a cord, which would prevent his leg being dislocated. He was feverish and spoke in snatches, possibly giving answers to questions heard inside his own head. I dozed off for a moment and it was his voice that roused me from my sleep: "It's all over for me now. But I can still shut my eyes and picture myself walking along beside a river.

And in the distance this woman moving ever onwards, halting from time to time and lighting a fire, and I don't even need to know where she's going . . ."

Ratinsky was still asleep in his "command post" when I settled Vassin onto the raft and handed him a pole and two paddles, roughly carved. A mile and a half from our camp the river flowed into the Amgun. I sought to reassure him: "There are no more rapids, I've checked."

He smiled: "If the worst comes to the worst, I'll just end up in the Pacific . . ."

He held out his pack to me. "Listen, Pavel. This has my boots in it, a saw, fifteen feet of cord, some smoked fish and ten dry biscuits. And my mug. When I've gone, walk down to the ford, and cross the river . . . No, the girl won't shoot at you. Throw the pack to her and come back here quickly. If you have problems with Ratinsky, tell him she stole my stuff."

Without giving me time to react, he took out a knife, released the bottom of his uniform jacket, where it was held in by his belt, and cut into the cloth. His hand hacked away at it and the cut ran round his body, creating a long strip of fabric. "And this as well! For her feet . . ."

He tossed this ribbon to me, thrust the pole into the sand and pushed off. The current bore him away into the darkness. For just a few seconds I could hear the lapping of the water against the vessel that carried him.

*

"He's gone? Good riddance! I prefer to have plenty of elbow room."

Ratinsky appeared energetic and resolute, like a general just before a battle. "We mustn't cock this up now. What's in it for me is another star on my epaulettes. And a mention in dispatches for you, Gartsev, or even a medal. As the girl can't walk away anymore, her tactic is going to be to hole up somewhere and fire at us from that vantage point. We'll catch her in a pincer movement and then, hey presto, a rope around her neck and she'll bite the dust. Then, we'll see . . . If she's not too ugly, we can polish her arse for her, the little bitch, ha, ha!"

He was excited now, affecting both the command headquarters jargon that Luskas was fond of and the rough soldier's banter of Butov. The puny little adolescent in him was going to have his revenge.

We crossed the river just as the day was dawning. I was afraid that Ratinsky might notice the footprints I had left when carrying Vassin's pack over to near where the fugitive spent the night. But he was too excited by the idea of the attack. Sending me ahead on an encircling manoeuvre, he was himself progressing from tree to tree, going down on one knee to take aim at spots he considered might be hiding the target – in short, rehearsing all the exercises from his army training.

When I got there shortly after him – he had not wanted to share his moment of triumph – I found him beside the camp fire, his revolver describing wild circles . . . The woman was no longer there.

"But we didn't see her getting away! The plan to surround

her was flawless. It's as if someone had warned her . . . Wait. So what's she been cooking?"

With the toe of his boot he stirred the embers . . . A shot threw up a cloud of ash. We flung ourselves to the ground, thinking we were being fired at. But no second bullet followed and, close to the fire, we found the case from a cartridge the fugitive had left "baking" in the ashes.

"It's a warning . . ." stammered Ratinsky, and I noticed that his lips were trembling. He must have seen his fear reflected in my eyes and quickly went back to playing the part of the hard man. "Right. She can't be far away, otherwise that cartridge would have gone off sooner."

After several minutes, emerging onto the bank of the stream, we caught sight of the familiar figure. I was sure that Ratinsky would immediately notice that the fugitive was wearing boots and walking more easily. He picked up nothing. In his head this woman, who was going to be captured, raped and handed over to the camp authorities, already belonged to the past. And the glorious future was the two lieutenant's stars, congratulations from the top brass, and finally marriage, settling into a "real life".

Mechanically he kept repeating, "Get a move on, Gartsev! Another five minutes and it'll all be over. Faster!"

This took no account of the fact that, well shod, the woman could now keep up the pace. She led us onto a marshy riverbank, managing to avoid it herself by taking a short cut through the forest, thus gaining a lead on us of a good three quarters of a mile. As dusk fell Ratinsky was forced to recognise this. "It doesn't matter. We'll catch her tomorrow morning. That way, we'll have a whole day for seeing to her." He threw me a wink, which was intended to be ribald, but in which I sensed a trace of unease . . .

The wind got up and we were now hunched against the lash of rain-swept branches. The taiga, sombre and hostile, let us through grudgingly. That night the canvas of our tent streamed and rattled under the squalls.

I fell asleep at once but, accustomed to remaining on the qui vive, I was woken by the sound of a moaning whisper. Without giving myself away by a movement or a sigh, I listened and was stunned to realise that what I could make out in the darkness was the muttered words of a prayer. Yes, Ratinsky was praying! The luminous face of his watch was tracing a sign of the cross . . . Did he notice my silence, which was too alert for someone asleep? His mumbling came to an end, he sighed and several minutes later I heard him snoring.

What kind of god had he just been invoking? The question plunged me into dazed perplexity. Yes, what could such a man be asking of heaven? And what was his faith? A tradition that his grandparents, diehard Polish Catholics, had handed down to him? Or did he have that very human habit of seeking the aid of some personal divinity concocted from odd bits and pieces?

"That's something I do myself sometimes . . ." I reflected rather grudgingly. But what had he been praying for? No doubt the capture of the fugitive and promotion to the rank of lieutenant . . . As for the pleasure of raping her, no, that certainly would not have come into his prayer. Nevertheless, the Almighty could not be unaware of the desire that inflamed the puny body of a certain Sub-Lieutenant Ratinsky.

Listening in the darkness to his tranquil breathing, I smiled. To despise him would have been unfair, for what he was asking in his prayer differed little from the things I had quite recently aspired to. As in my case, with Sveta, he hoped for a conjugal nest, the birth of a child. I remembered a trip with my fiancée to a furniture shop, where a massive wardrobe had inspired covetous longings in us. Which had not prevented me from continuing with my thesis on the Marxist vision of revolutionary violence . . . No, I did not consider myself to be in any way superior to this Ratinsky with his striving to get all the odds, God included, on his side. A chain of events had made me remote from the life he dreamed of. Sveta's betrayal ("No more massive wardrobes for me!" I thought with a silent chuckle). My coming to this far eastern end of the world. My interment in shelter number nineteen . . . And I thought again about what Vassin had spoken of: following in a woman's footsteps without questioning what the goal of her endless trek might be. The notion of embarking on such a journey, he had said, would have given him faith in something beyond the reality of our own lives . . .

In the middle of the night the wind subsided and a flood of moonlight lit up our tent. A scraping sound reached my ears. I sat up, thinking it might be an animal attracted by the remains of the fish we had discarded. I seized the rifle, slipped outside and, cocking an ear towards this repeated grating noise, I recognised the coming and going of a saw. The moon, virtually full, was spreading a phosphorescent blue patina over the sand on the riverbank. It was a bright enough light for selecting a tree and cutting it up . . .

Nervous of attracting Ratinsky's attention, I returned to my bed. He did not wake up but, through his sleep, enunciated with surprising clarity: "I did it, Mama. I promised you, and I did it . . ." As I wrapped my head in a square of fabric for protection against mosquitoes, I thought: "That's a little adolescent speaking . . . His god must have the features of a loving mother."

WE WERE ON GRADUALLY RISING TERRAIN, BUT THIS CHANGE of level did not become apparent until we had reached the top of a very steep riverbank and found ourselves peering down from the edge of this abrupt bluff . . .

Ratinsky was so surprised that he almost toppled over the brink of the sandy cliff, a drop of some thirty feet. He grew agitated, pulling faces in angry confusion. What I could now see was exactly what I had pictured during the night when I heard the scraping of a saw.

The fugitive was just pushing a raft out into the river, one that bore little resemblance to those Vassin had constructed. A much narrower craft and, no doubt, easier to handle on these endlessly sinuous waterways.

"We must stop her!" yelled Ratinsky. "Otherwise we'll never catch her!" Then he noticed the woman was well shod. "But those are Vassin's boots," came his strangled cry. "Who gave her those?"

He took out his revolver, rested it on his folded arm and fired. But at that distance the revolver was of little use.

"Shoot her, Gartsev!" he shouted, after his third bullet had gone astray. "Hit her in the legs!"

The fugitive, up to her ankles in the water, was struggling with the weight of the raft, sliding it over the sand with difficulty.

Taking my time, I loaded the rifle, and aimed it. "But, Comrade Sub-Lieutenant, what if, by ill luck, my aim goes astray and I kill her?" I thus gained a few seconds, pretending to be concerned about the orders we had been given.

"I don't give a shit about that! The main thing is not to let her get away . . ."

My shot raised a little flurry of sand beside the raft. The next bullet caused a spurt of water. Ratinsky snatched the rifle from me, took aim . . . His shot sliced a fragment of wood off the raft. "No, we must get closer to her," he yelled in fury. "This blunderbuss is hopelessly inaccurate!"

We rushed over to a spot where the riverbank was not so high, hurtled down the slope and managed to draw close to the woman before she had got onto the raft. Ratinsky was emptying his cartridge clip as he ran, but missing the target. "Fire, Gartsev, aim for the belly!" We were no more than fifty paces away from the woman. I was sure I could get to her. "Comrade Sub-Lieutenant, we could arrest her now, without wounding her."

At these words Ratinsky became beside himself. He sprang at me and the barrel of his revolver grazed my cheek. "I tell you, fire!" He was foaming at the mouth, his eyes drilling into me with hatred. With one hand he was still rummaging about in his cartridge pouch to find another clip. "Fire!"

I had no time to obey. The shot rang out and I thought he was the one who had just inadvertently fired. Bizarrely, he shook his revolver, as if disgusted, and threw it down onto the sand. A second later I realised what had happened.

Close by the raft the woman was holding her rifle. Her bullet had pierced Ratinsky's hand and he was now yelling, nursing his right arm the way one holds a baby. The palm of his hand was bleeding.

Almost at once he started weeping, and his moaning would continue throughout the time it took to prepare for his departure. I washed his wound and then washed it again, disinfecting it with alcohol he had surreptitiously stored away during our drinking bouts and which he was keeping in a flask Butov thought he had lost. It took all the dressings we had left to bandage him. The bullet had struck neither the bones nor the joints and, in principle, he was in a fit state to continue our trek. But, in his view, his life was in danger and only medical treatment could save him. His talk was a farrago of tetanus, septicaemia and reduced haemoglobin.

Fully occupied by treating his wound, we had forgotten the fugitive. And when I saw that the raft had not moved from where it lay beside the river I could not believe my eyes. As for the woman, she had disappeared; all one could see was her footprints, following the shoreline, then leading up into the forest.

"I order you to continue the pursuit." Ratinsky's decision both concerned and delighted me. Staring at me suspiciously, he added: "And it will be in your interests not to be too friendly with the escaped prisoner! And certainly not to supply her with boots and tools . . ."

Thinking of the solution we had now used several times, I suggested he leave by water: "Comrade Sub-Lieutenant, we don't even need to construct a raft. The girl has left us with hers . . ." He would not hear of it. "No, I shall return on foot. I'll walk along beside this river and then follow the Amgun . . ." I tried to insist but in vain, and finally he admitted, "I can't swim, Gartsev."

His fear gave him an almost touching air. As did his arm, which he was nursing, snivelling all the while. I sought to encourage him. "Well, after all, it may be even quicker on foot. You won't have all those bends in the small rivers to negotiate. We've done a lot of moving around without making much progress. But our training area isn't all that far away, thirty miles at most . . . And you have the maps . . ."

He set off the same day. I watched his little figure walking along the riverbank. I was hoping, I could not tell why, that I might see him turning back to wave me goodbye. But he must already have been putting the finishing touches to the report he would be presenting to Luskas: his brilliant strategy, his heroic wound . . . What role would he assign to me in his account? The truth was that he was leaving me behind in the taiga to conceal the failure of the operation. And when I returned I would be a ready-made scapegoat.

In the eyes of his god?

V

I DID NOT HAVE TO DO TOO MUCH TRACKING TO CATCH up with the fugitive before nightfall. Indeed, she had not been seeking to evade me as she walked on upstream beside the river. The evening was warmed by the breeze coming from the south, from the Sea of Japan, I told myself, picturing a land with a sub-tropical climate as the source of this late summer breeze.

Soon her three fires were alight. In the corner of a wooded fold in the ground I could make out her silhouette moving back and forth in front of the flames.

"Is she thinking about me, about how I'm waiting out here in the darkness?" For the first time this question crossed my mind. Previously there had been several of us and I could only presume that she regarded us all in the same way: with fear, disgust and a wish to escape from this pack of sometimes cowardly, sometimes aggressive soldiers.

From now on, there was only me, a man worn out by the chase, by lack of sleep, by insufficient food. Like her, I had lit a fire and prepared a meal and I sat there unmoving, my gaze lost in the flames. I was inhaling the same air laden with southern softness, hearing the same monotonous cry of a bird as it flew over both our camps. Each of us was aware of these intimate moments, adrift amid the mighty, indeterminate time of the taiga.

I had never before been linked to someone by such an evident bond. The woman was there and her presence sufficed to transform the instant I was living in. A nocturnal revelation to which she and I were simple witnesses. The subtle advent of an unknown world. I tried to find words for it, reaching out in my mind towards the discovery of some hidden meaning, the foretaste of some mystery . . . But such words, derived from my complex and rational past, only served to obscure what no longer needed explanation. It was enough to think (and I was certain she was thinking it, too) that she and I could have stood up and walked towards one another, solely to exchange glances, attesting to what we had just understood.

Once again I pictured the gate leading to a dwelling lost deep in the forest. Except that this time I could already see myself actually crossing the threshold, with my hand still on the door.

Fear returned when, on waking and turning back the canvas of my tent, I found the edges welded together. During the night the wind had swung round to the north, turning the humid air from the ocean into solid ice. I tugged on the fabric, rigid as sheet metal; the crust broke and it took me a moment to recognise my surroundings.

A blue hoar frost gave the forest a haughty aspect, indifferent to my need to live at the heart of it. This kingdom of ice seemed to be turning its back on me.

My food – what was left of the remaining smoked taimen, prepared by Vassin – was frozen hard, and, as I swallowed rough mouthfuls of it, I could not resist an impulsive reaction: a shiver of pleasure at the thought of a clean, warm apartment, with a well-stocked kitchen and a real bed. That shared moment of the night before, the bond linking me to the presence of the fugitive, all that was broken. I was once more a soldier charged with a mission, for which the reward would be a return to his old life.

The ground, now white, revealed footprints more clearly. Those of the woman, but, especially, the varied tracks left by animals. I thought I could see where a fox had passed, or was it the paws of a wolf? And this? A lynx perhaps? As an illiterate in this environment that was hard to read, I reckoned that my chances of surviving for long were poor. What terrified me about a bear's footprint was the depth of the incisions left by its claws. It had passed this way only shortly before, I told myself, as I tried to improve my reading skills. Yes, fresh prints, left since the frost came. What could have attracted it towards our two camps? Was it our food supplies, or our human flesh? At this time of year was it already looking for a den where it could hibernate, or was it stuffing itself, building up as much fat as possible with which to face the nine months of ice and snow?

Now thick with frost, the grass was no longer concealing the dangers, spelled out by these autographs on the forest floor.

During the course of that day a pair of wolves had several times crossed my path. Sometimes behind me, sometimes passing in front of me.

The fugitive seemed no longer to be taking any notice of me. Instead of following a tortuous path, as formerly, in order to confuse us, she was heading north now, and only deviating from this course to avoid the occasional marsh or river that could not be forded.

One evening I heard a gunshot, a single bullet, as when she had fired at Luskas, Butov or Ratinsky. A thought crossed my mind: one of these days she was going to eliminate the scarcely dangerous but persistent pursuer that I was. One shot, my body slumps down, pain, darkness. And the predators arrive, whose signatures on the hoar frost I lacked the knowledge to decipher.

An hour later I detected the smell of grilled meat on the air.

I was well aware of her survival skills: the fugitive was at home here in the taiga! That was why she had outmanoeuvred us for so long. Every pine needle here was her ally. And our enemy.

My own course mimicked the path she took down to the last detour. Afraid of getting lost, I would set up my camp for the night as close as possible to hers, not in order to launch an attack but so as not to lose sight of her.

My reserves of food were exhausted. I tried to hunt, like her. During one halt at the edge of a fir plantation, I caught sight of a cluster of birds. They looked like capercaillies but their dark plumage was flecked with white. (I would later learn these were hazel grouse.) They were making their way through the undergrowth, pecking at berries and uttering brief guttural sounds . . . Then I realised just how famished I was. I had the urge to leap at one of them, tear it to pieces and swallow its flesh raw. I aimed at the closest of them and fired . . . But it was another bird, surrounded by its chicks, that was hit, uttered a harrowing cry and fled into the bushes (I had long since forgotten that the sights of the rifle had been distorted by Vassin). I wasted an hour looking for that wounded bird. In vain. The thought of it in its death throes in a thicket made me forget my hunger.

That was the day when I began coughing and shivering in clothes that gave poor protection against the biting wind. We had set off at the beginning of August and now, three weeks later, the cold came sweeping through the little Edens of warmth that still lingered in the sunlit valleys . . .

I faced a dilemma with few options. I could either walk on, without food, and let myself be caught by the snow, which would soon be falling. Or else turn back, with the idea of reaching Amgun before the real frosts arrived. And die all the same, getting lost in a network of waterways that would soon be iced over.

Realising this deprived me of sleep. I chewed on a handful of berries, my only food for two days now.

It was a calm, richly starlit night. The fires lit by the fugitive glowed feebly. I got up and took a few steps towards these embers . . .

A shadowy figure moved across, hiding one of the fires. Visibly, the woman was on her feet and getting ready to leave. The thought terrified me. She was going away in secret, leaving me alone, incapable of finding the way, worn out by fever, lacking in food . . . My fingers stiff with cold and anxiety, I dismantled the tent, attached it to my pack, and set off. My harsh, barking cough could be heard over a long distance in the silence of the taiga.

My face scratched by twigs and branches, I reached the site of the woman's camp. Three little mounds of embers and complete darkness all around, no indication of which way she had gone.

My legs would no longer support me. Collapsing beside one of the fires, I could feel that the ground was warm. A couch had been rigged up here at this spot and beneath an armful of fir branches there were embers, well and truly extinguished, but which gave off dry, slow warmth. I lay down there and suddenly sat up, detecting the aroma of roast meat. My blocked nose dulled my sense of smell, but, driven by violent hunger, I rummaged amid the remains of a fire . . .

What I discovered was unhoped for: the carcass of a bird, half charred, but from which my teeth could pick off fragments of meat that crunched deliciously in my mouth.

When I got up to move on, my hunger satisfied, the blind alley that awaited me became all too clear once more. The hunt was going to exhaust me and finish me off. But if I turned back and, by some miracle, found my way, I would simply be returning empty-handed and playing the part Luskas had already written for me: that of a deserter who had given clothing and weapons to the escaped prisoner. And who knows what further accusations he might have dreamed up by then!

The only solution, therefore, as before, was to capture the woman. The meat I had eaten had given me renewed energy. In order to break free from the taiga, yes, to "escape" in my turn, I felt capable of attacking the fugitive, even killing her.

The brightness of the morning enabled me to make up for lost time. Emerging onto a small lake I stopped: the woman was walking along slowly and seemed little concerned by the fact that I was following in her footsteps. My warlike energy flagged, my illness returned, making my head feel hot and heavy and lacerating my lungs with an increasingly harsh cough. Through my torpor, a plaintive voice, that of the "rag doll" was begging: "Please don't let her go any faster. And, most of all, let her allow herself to be captured! I want to go home. I want to go back to life the way it was."

I no longer had the strength to feel contempt for that inner voice of mine.

THE FOLLOWING MORNING I DRAGGED MYSELF OVER TO the campsite the fugitive had just left. The remnants of her meal were more abundant this time: part of a hare's carcass, boletus mushrooms baking in the ashes and, abandoned on some dead leaves covered in frost, a piece of taimen. I ate everything, reclining on a couch of branches whose wood held the warmth of extinguished embers. As on the day before, the strength I regained was fiercely directed towards this single goal: capturing the fugitive, which would give me back a clean, healthy life, all my desires satisfied.

We were still heading north. Dressed in her grey prisoner's smock, the woman did not seem to be suffering from the chill gusts that froze my chest. She sometimes seemed to pause when, thanks to a peat bog or the absence of a ford, she had to change course and plunge back into the forest. These hesitations were my salvation, each one allowing me to gain several dozen yards.

As night fell, the distance between us was so reduced that I believed I would at last be able to launch an attack on her. I broke into a run, choking on my cough, my eyes swimming, my temples throbbing. Although I was taking long strides, I felt as if I were running on the spot ...

It took me several minutes to realise that the path led uphill and that trying to run among dwarf pine trees could result only in this painful shuffle. When the track turned a corner I stumbled, catching at one of the little twisted trunks, and fell, my eyes fixed on the woman who was unhurriedly moving on ...

This halt brought me a desperate lucidity. I admitted to myself that the aim of this last attempt had been a resolution at all costs, yes, even at the cost of my death, which would have occurred had I charged the escaped prisoner. She would have put a bullet through my head, or through my leg, to leave me to rot here, waiting for some beast of prey to come by. My attack was a suicide attempt in disguise.

Now she was moving further away, leaving me alone – this wreck of a man who could no longer stand upright, with scant hope of finding the strength to crawl as far as some unlikely camping ground.

Her figure was getting smaller. One step followed another and already the dusk was drawing a veil over the gentle rhythm of her gait. In my fevered imagination I was picturing the space that would be left amid the trees after she had disappeared ...

Suddenly it seemed to me that she was no longer moving forward! I hauled myself up, holding on to a branch, and focused on her more sharply ... No, the woman had come to a standstill, appearing to hesitate over which direction to take. I started walking towards her, using my rifle as a stick.

At this moment she turned and, improbably, gave the impression that she was waiting for me.

I regained the usual distance between us, one it would take for the sound of a voice, or rather that of my cough, to carry. The fugitive veered off towards a hollow, thick with spruce. Half an hour later, as if she had guessed that I was at the end of my tether, she stopped for the night.

I hastened to find a spot that was sheltered from the wind but would allow me to keep an eye on her fires.

Somewhat away from the track, I stepped over a little ditch, beat a path for myself through some tall bracken turned russet by the frosts, and all of a sudden, found myself looking, wide-eyed, at the timber walls of a hunting lodge!

I felt a cosy thrill at the prospect of sleeping under a roof. I followed the wall round, feeling my way, found the door, went in and struck a match, which gave me just enough time to see a straw mattress in the corner and let myself collapse onto it.

I woke often, afraid of missing the fugitive's departure. Several times I forced myself to thrust my head outside, amid an icy wind, for a quick look at her campfires through the swaying of the branches.

My sleep was sometimes broken by the disturbing sensation of being watched by someone – a mute presence in the depths of this narrow shelter . . .

I had bursts of fever when my thoughts became confused, blending together overlapping fragments of speech, faces that encroached on one another. I heard Butov's voice, holding forth during one of our drinking bouts, after our attempt to rape the escaped prisoner. Aware of our ignominy, he was muttering: "That's what turns us all into a herd – our perpetual desire for a fuck. Our rulers don't need to carry a whip. They've got us by the balls. We're afraid of giving up our little pleasures and so we're willing to obey any old bastard . . ." With a troubled smile, Vassin was whispering: "You need to reach rock bottom, Pavel. It's the best thing that can happen to a man. After my first year in prison that was the freedom I began to experience. Yes, freedom! They could send me to a camp with a more brutal regime, torture me, kill me. Their world didn't concern me, because it was only a game and I was no longer playing. To play, you had to be filled with desire, hatred, fear. But these were no longer cards I held in my hand. I was free . . ."

I dozed off and the faces faded. All that remained was the troubling certainty of a gaze fixed on me in the darkness. Getting up, I half opened the door, checked that the fugitive's fires were still alight, lay down again. And, as if in response to Vassin, I asked myself if my inability to carry on walking was not the way out of the game he had been talking about.

At about five o'clock in the morning I made ready to depart. Outside, the triangle of embers was still glowing, the rain had ceased and the taiga maintained a massive, frozen silence. All the heat in the universe seemed to be concentrated in my burning throat as I gasped for breath.

I lit a match, managed to revive the wick of a melted candle in a food tin, withdrew the rest of my food from my pack, ate.

It was as I was getting up that I unintentionally cast light into a corner of the room . . .

I did not drop the candle, I did not flee from the building. I stood there with the back of my neck pressed against the door frame, very likely imitating the expression of the figure that was staring at me.

A corpse, seated with its back to the wall, its legs stretched out, its arms sprawled across the floor. Its waxy and emaciated face was that of a mummy. Its bluish white hair stirred imperceptibly – as did its clothes – on account of the insects that must have been disturbed by the light.

Its left leg was caught by the ankle in a great iron clamp – a bear trap. Being totally dried out, the man's body did not seem to have been subject to decay. His face even retained a certain expression, a sharp grimace, and appeared animated, despite his empty eye sockets. His lowered chin gave him the appearance of someone contemplating the state of his body and, in particular, his ankle, crushed between the jaws of the trap.

Coming to my senses, I noticed a thick canvas bag lying there, a little to one side. I reached out with the barrel of my rifle and poked about in the frayed fabric. Little gleaming grains spilled out slowly onto the ground. Gold, I thought, recalling with a vague renewal of interest what this metal means to men. I reversed the rifle and, not without a feeling of sacrilege, struck a blow with the butt against the trap . . .

With a crash the great set of steel dentures sprang towards me. I jumped clear. The screw that held the rusty spring in place had just given way. Displaced by the jolt, the corpse had swivelled sideways and was now looking towards the door.

I blew out the candle and ventured into the darkness. My eyes were blinded at first, but then I could once more make out the three red spots of the camp beyond the trees. I no longer knew why I was continuing to follow these fires. The corpse had just shown me what was going to happen to me. Except that, in my case, the trap would not be those spring-loaded jaws but the whole of the taiga and the icy closing-in of its nights. This corpse was how I was going to end up. So what it inspired in me was not revulsion but, rather, a strange understanding.

The frosty grass crunched beneath my feet, an arctic breeze had arrived during the night. Yet I no longer felt cold and the branches lashing my face gave rise to feelings almost of tenderness in me – a caress after my long solitary wanderings.

The snow began falling at the moment when, unsteady on my feet, I reached the camp of the woman I still believed was the object of my pursuit.

She was not there and, with an indifference that surprised even myself, I grasped that this surge of white was going to cover her tracks. This realisation, resigned as it was, fuelled an ultimate will to survive within me – the "rag doll" became alarmed, infected me with its fear, urging me to act.

"Why not call out to her?" I thought, framing this cry in my mind: "Help! I'm lost! I want to . . ." But the truth was that all I wanted was to get back to my old life, my "rag doll's" life.

There was no food lying about near the fire. Wrapping myself up in the hardened sides of the tent, I managed to construct a vague cocoon. I revived one of the fires, melted some snow in my mug, ate my last fragments.

The swirling of the snowflakes became thicker, blotting out the forest. I told myself that freezing to death would be like falling asleep painlessly … It would, of course, have made sense to go back to the hunting lodge, much better sheltered from the elements. I even ventured on a moment of hope: with the half dozen cartridges I still had left, I could hunt, get back on my feet again … But then the memory of the desiccated corpse came back to me. In broad daylight I felt I would be unable to bear its gaze. Besides, moving back there would have changed nothing. The chances of being rescued by the military district authorities were slim. And I no longer had enough strength to shoot animals, cut wood … or attempt a return … I became aware of this, without emotion, thrust another branch into the fire, began falling asleep.

And I failed to notice that the light was already fading and another night was coming.

I CAN DISTINCTLY REMEMBER MY LAST THOUGHT BEFORE I lost consciousness. In trying to cover up my body with the few garments I possessed, I managed to wrap the top half warmly but left my legs out in the cold. In covering my head, I had left my back bare. I could still be aware of the ridiculous aspect of my contortions but no longer had the courage to emerge from my canvas sheath, break off branches, feed the fire. This slide into unconsciousness was a gentle one, all suffering seemed to be already behind me.

It was a brief twinge of pain that woke me. From childhood onwards, I had known this burning sensation: a child puts his frozen hands under a stream of hot water and cries out as the blood comes rushing back too violently into his fingers . . .

I now felt just such a gnawing pain in my left arm, the one that had been the most exposed to the cold and was now, inexplicably, feeling a surge of warmth. Pushing back the piece of canvas that was covering my head, I saw that my fire was still burning brightly, keeping the darkness at bay, so it was the blaze of it that was bringing me back to life.

For several minutes this flow of heat built up within me

and I drank it in with my numb lips. Then I sat up on my couch, and became aware of the little clearing, already covered in snow, watched over by a mute, austere ring of trees.

A brief crackle could be heard behind me. I swung round and in my mental confusion I imagined that the corpse had left its shelter and had made its way to this spot . . .

What I saw was almost more alarming: some ten yards away there was a little fire burning between two larch trees, and a human shape, with its back to me, huddled in front of the flames. The folds of the canvas sheet that covered it made it impossible to identify, but I knew it could only be the fugitive.

Everything I was about to do came together in my mind in a sequence of obvious actions. Capture her, go back to the training area, a happy return to my old life . . . Instinct suggested it would be best not to reach for my rifle: in loading it, I should have woken the woman who, being more agile, would have anticipated my shot. No, I must seize her gun, threaten her, wound her if necessary . . .

My sleep and the warmth had summoned up within me that reserve of strength that the body keeps for life and death moments. I disengaged myself from my cocoon, sat up, and, bracing my muscles, jumped to my feet and made a dash towards the escaped prisoner . . .

And fell close beside her, my hand reaching for her rifle. Dazed with terror, I became aware that my left ankle was caught in a noose that was fastened to a tree root.

The woman got up slowly, picked up a brand and, coming over to me, shone its light on my face. Too terrified, all I could do was note the severe beauty of her features and a scar on her chin, the mark left by Ratinsky's bullet.

In her gaze hostility gave way to sadness, even compassion, which I recognised from the trembling at the corners of her mouth and the slight shaking of her head, a look that informed me of the state I was in. It seemed to me that it was a very long time since I had known such an expression of shared sorrow. Not since my childhood, perhaps, in my mother's lifetime.

I tried to speak, thinking I could anticipate her questions. She made a sign with her hand to show me she had no need of my excuses. And furthermore, my voice was already choking in a painful, eviscerating cough. The illness I had been able to hold in check at the moment of that failed assault was returning, burning my lungs, inflaming my breath. I found it hard to make out the fugitive's gestures, aware only that she was helping me to stand up.

We moved slowly away from that spot, which would have been too easy to locate on account of the gold washer's hut. Understanding the reason for our walk enabled me to remain upright in the course of that snowy morning.

During a halt the woman made me eat some roasted meat and got me to swallow a very hot drink. I felt a smile and also tears appearing on my face, as if it were someone else's . . . Then the sky grew dark and I could no longer tell if it was dusk falling or my perception of an imminent loss of consciousness.

I came to in the middle of the night, disturbed by a rough carapace scratching my chest every time I breathed in. Uneasily

I thrust my hand inside my tunic and my fingers encountered a strange substance, like a fleece coated with glue. I propped myself up on one elbow, wanting to rid myself of this hair shirt, it was scratching my skin so much, but the woman's voice murmured: "Leave it . . . It's prickly, but it's doing you good . . ."

The embers spread out across the ground gave a faint light to our refuge: my two tents that the fugitive had fitted together, folding back the canvas at the bottom, so as to be able to attend to the fire. An aluminium mug was warming there – Vassin's, it occurred to me with a pang. The woman followed my gaze, picked up the mug, and held it to my lips. I recognised the bittersweet brew that had soothed my cough: a thick infusion that gave off a smell of resin and made my tongue smart.

Letting myself fall back onto my bed of branches, I studied the "Tungus woman" with grievous attention, as if her expression could have explained to me everything that had happened and what she intended to do with me. Her features remained impassive: slanting eyes, prominent Asiatic cheekbones, lips fixed in a line of silence. Her hair had grown back a little more and its sleek blackness now concealed the contours of her skull . . .

She picked up my mug again, filled it with snow, put it back on the embers. Then, without a word, she removed the "hair shirt" laid across my chest and I saw that it was a slab of moss, dried and heated over the fire. She spread it out across a grid of fine branches held over the embers, allowed it to heat up and, once more, slipped it beneath my tunic. A warm wave of well-being surged through me. I breathed in carefully, for fear of setting off a coughing fit. Sleep prolonged what I was now experiencing: a feeling that I existed far away from this body that was clinging on to survival, far from my past, far from the world of other people, where I no longer had any part to play.

ON THE FOURTH DAY WE RESUMED OUR JOURNEY. THE FIRST offensive of the snows had delivered a warning and then retreated, giving way to misty, autumnal weather that granted the trees and animals enough time to prepare for the blizzards and great frosts of true winter.

Round about noon a humid and gentle breeze brought a slight flavour of salt to my lips. I felt as if I were emerging from a long fainting fit and, as my strength returned, I could no longer manage to silence this insistently recurring thought: "So who is now compelling me to follow her, this woman?"

I went on walking behind her, as if our goals had become the same. Hills, slopes, fords. I pictured how easy it would have been for me to slow down, to turn round without being seen, to retrace our path in the opposite direction and be back at the training area within a week . . . The idea obsessed me. Our arduous progress through the twisted pine trees of a stlanik brought home to me the absurdity of this trek. I remembered that day when I had come across a darned smock and knew the escaped prisoner was close at hand. I had not betrayed her, I had saved her life. Just as she had now saved mine in curing me. Thus we were quits!

My only motive for staying with her was one of selfish timidity: I was not sure I could find my way back.

Yes, the "rag doll" still lived within me.

Marking time on the sand of a riverbank, I began to allow myself to fall behind the fugitive. She did not notice and was soon some thirty yards ahead of me. I saw her making her way – alone, silent, a slim figure following the course of a river in whose waters were reflected the dark crenellations of the forest and a gilded cloud . . . Vassin's words resounded within me, with their calm certainty: day after day, following a woman who knows nothing of your existence, as you know nothing of her destination, living only for this unending walk, asking for nothing else. For a brief moment I was intoxicated by the inspiring madness of this dream. I was already living it, and with extra intensity too, for the woman did know I was following her and seemed happy with this.

She began climbing up a slope. I stuck close behind her. The dream had passed and I was no longer able to find the slightest logic in this adventure: yet another hill to scramble up, bruising my feet against tree roots, battling with thickets. And then what?

On this occasion the ascent seemed to me interminable. The prospect of reaching a hilltop and then hurtling down the slope on the other side filled me with despair. "No, enough is enough," I kept saying to myself, feeling increasingly exasperated. "She must tell me her intentions." The "rag doll" within me counselled caution: I had no idea what the woman had in mind, it might be better to hint at my return obliquely, without provoking her . . .

I tried hard to catch up with her, so as to engage her, when we next halted, in a conversation that would resolve matters. Possibly sensing this, she stopped, and it was then that I saw the line of the ridge or, rather, the flat summit of the hill – visibly, our path was going to continue on the far slope.

All out of breath, I caught up with the woman, and was preparing to tell her that I intended to leave. But before I could speak she declared, in tones that could not conceal a certain hesitation, so improbable was what she was saying: "This is it . . . We've arrived . . ."

Her eyes were shining, misty with tears. I thought she was talking about our halt for the night and failed to understand why this choice of location upset her so much. I was on the point of flinging the roll of our tents down on the ground, but she caught me by the hand and drew me over to a spur of rock that crowned the hill. I went with her reluctantly.

What I saw, when we got up there, was impossible to express. Infinity, nothingness, a plunge into the void . . . My mind reached for such words, but they were eclipsed by the vertiginous beauty that had no need of them. The horizon was veiled by a light mist. The ocean, united with the sky, was the only element that surrounded us on all sides. And the sun, already low, reinforced this sensation of fusion, veiling everything with a gilded, dusty haze, making it impossible for the eye to focus on any detail. We were, I could see now, at the culminating point of a little promontory and the height of this location created an effect of being suspended aloft above the immensity of the ocean.

"That's where I have to go . . ." the woman told me, indicating the watery expanse.

The notion that she was going mad struck me forcibly. But perhaps she had been all along . . . And I should really have believed that, had not the dots of several tiny islands suddenly become clearly defined amid the glittering of the waters. One of them, with an irregular outline, seemed close to the shore.

"And you?" Still gazing into the distance, the fugitive put her question in tones that sought to be almost non-committal. "You want to go back home, is that it?"

I could have tried to explain that the sheer vastness of what lay before us terrified me. That this was a place where no human being could ever lead a reasonable existence, a "social" life. That, as a child, I had long ago witnessed the savage power of the elements, yes, the unbridled fury of the river that had killed my parents . . . Reasons more truthful than those I came out with haltingly, the falseness of which sickened me: my duty as a soldier, the concern of my nearest and dearest (I invented a family for myself), my work at the university . . .

She listened to me while preparing our shelter for the night. Or rather, she no longer listened to me. During our meal she spoke little and when I tried to question her about her past and the future she had in mind, her answers were vague. "Prison? I'm here to avoid going back there . . . Is it hard to survive in the taiga? Not as hard as in a camp . . ."

I already knew her forename, Elkan. I knew she belonged to the Nigidale people, local to the area. But when I asked her what her surname was, she observed softly: "For an escaped prisoner a number's enough, isn't it?"

I slept little, apprehensive of an outcome that seemed to me increasingly likely: the fugitive gets up, without waking me, takes possession of both of our rifles and disappears, abandoning me in this deserted spot. Or else she puts a bullet in my head before leaving!

But, in fact, she was getting on with things in a calm, routine fashion. I saw her bringing armfuls of branches to revive the fires, greasing her boots with the skin of a taimen and stitching a garment by the light of the flames . . .

In the morning I was woken by a metallic clicking sound. I looked out. She had taken a stone and was sharply tapping the barrel of my rifle. She finished off by raising it to her shoulder, taking aim at a tree and firing. A snapped twig fell down onto the layer of dead leaves.

I feigned a casual yawn. "So, is it in working order, my old blunderbuss?" Without looking at me, she replied: "It works now. The sights had been distorted. You'll need to be able to aim straight to feed yourself on your . . . return journey." Her voice faltered as she uttered these words. She quickly rallied. "Sit down. I'm going to show you the way."

Carefully, she unfolded a broad roll of bark stripped from the trunk of a birch tree. The route was marked on it using a quill from a bird. The "ink" came from the juice of berries crushed in her mug. A pinkish trace showed the succession of tributaries of the Amgun, the fords, the landmarks . . . And the marshy areas to avoid. The simplicity of the whole rough map worried me.

"Are you sure it's as easy as that?" I asked, trying not to sound too suspicious. "On the way here, I felt as if we were wandering around endlessly in a maze."

She gave me a hard look. "On the way here, I had to mix up all the pathways to survive . . . If you walk at a good pace, it'll take you four or five days, at most."

I gathered up my rifle, now made good, one of the tents, some smoked fish and that mixture of wild rose hips and spruce shoots that had helped to cure me. Elkan handed me an extensive cape. I now guessed she had been making it during the night, using the groundsheet from our tents. "The hood comes off," she explained. "That can be handy, at times . . ."

I needed to say goodbye and leave quickly before she changed her mind. The "rag doll", my jittery guardian angel, was urging me to go now. Overridden by its timorous babble, another voice was meanwhile spelling out the real reason for my hesitation, a feeling altogether different from that of fear.

"What are you going to tell your . . . superiors?" Elkan suddenly asked me, still giving me a hard look.

"Well . . . I'll say I lost sight of you and that . . . as winter was closing in, I had to turn back . . ."

"They'll accuse you of letting me go free and you'll be put in prison."

Her certainty made me uneasy.

"What else can I say? It's the truth. After all, I could have abandoned the chase and gone back long ago . . ."

"But you didn't. Why not?"

Her voice was muted, concealing her hope for an answer that would have had nothing to do with the manhunt and the world I was planning to return to. This was perhaps the moment when I became more intimately aware than ever of her presence: this bruised life, one I could touch with my hand, this pale, fine face, scarred by a bullet, reaching out to me, hoping for a response from me, her eyes focused on me with a glint of distraught tenderness. Yes, with a gentleness I had not known since childhood.

I had a sense now of why I was hesitating to leave . . . while within my heart the "rag doll" was squirming.

"I'll simply tell my superior officers that I did everything I could to capture you and that in the end I fell ill and . . ."

Elkan interrupted me in a voice which, though severe, still, for a moment, retained its note of tenderness.

"No, they won't believe you. You must tell them . . . that you shot me . . . when crossing a river. My body was swept away. Impossible to retrieve it. Yes, I'm dead. That's what you'll tell them. Safe journey . . ."

She turned her back on me and began walking down the hillside towards the shore.

The last sight I had of her was of her silhouette, outlined against the endless expanse of the ocean.

ELKAN HAD CALCULATED THE DURATION OF THE JOURNEY correctly: it was going to take less than five days for me to return to the training area.

The calm, mild weather would almost have been reminiscent of spring had it not been for all the foliage, turned russet by the frosts of the preceding days. I made rapid progress, tramping along the sand of the riverbanks with the energy of an athlete in the run-up to a jump.

The map on the birch bark, though very makeshift, showed what was most important, the bends in the route and the length of each stage. I ate little, did not halt at all during the day, and every morning set out on the road from the first light of dawn. The taiga was closing behind me like the curtain falling on a life now definitely at an end.

Naturally, reminders of our escapade, on the outward journey, cropped up from time to time. I recognised the hill where I had interrupted the escaped prisoner in her needlework. And the bank where Vassin had buried his dog . . . But these memories simply served as landmarks that I noted, situated and forgot.

The more I ran over in my mind the version of events that

the fugitive had suggested – her death – the more convincing this lie seemed to me and the harder to refute. A hot pursuit, a shot fired as we crossed a ford, her body swept away towards the rapids by the current. The story was writing itself in my head, I could hear it being recited in the febrile tones of the "rag doll". This guarantor of my desire to survive was keeping a weather eye open, anticipating trick questions, doubt, suspicion. My tale seemed unassailable: I aim, I fire, I kill and, thanks to the force of the current, my prey escapes me. At all events, how could I have dragged her through the taiga for dozens of miles?

Thus, in the end, it was I who was the hero of the operation! I was returning to report that the mission had been accomplished, which made up for all our setbacks. I began quite seriously to envisage receiving Butov's congratulations, perhaps even a medal. And going home to Leningrad would be like a happy recovery after a long night of fever.

In a dream I had a vision of the person I had almost turned into. I was lying stark naked in the snow and all around my body a woman was lighting flickering fires which kept being extinguished by flurries of snow. She battled on in her struggle against the cold, each time a spark flew out it secured a brief moment of survival for me. And, as is often the case in mute, violent dreams like this, I failed to say what was most important. That these actions, in their tender self-denial, were a part of a life unknown to me, but the only one in which I longed to believe . . .

I REACHED THE TRAINING AREA JUST AFTER MIDNIGHT. IN the hut at the checkpoint the sentry levelled his gun at me as if at a ghost, then, emerging from his daze, growled: "Yes . . . I've been told . . . But I've got to call the guard sergeant."

The latter appeared and stared at me with an air both intrigued and suspicious. "Captain Luskas' orders are . . . Yes, to put you under arrest. Hand over your weapon and follow me."

I stammered out explanations, said there must be some mistake and insisted that Major Butov should be informed at once . . . He did not listen to me, muttering: "I've got my orders. Quick march!"

The duty guard's rifle prodded me in the back, the sergeant began marching. I could only follow behind him.

They led me to one of the anti-atomic shelters, made me go down the steps and closed the heavy trapdoor . . . In the darkness I sat down on a pallet, not feeling too anxious, telling myself that in the morning, when I told Luskas I had shot down the fugitive, I would be freed, rehabilitated, even rewarded.

I was about to lie down when I heard a click, and the flame of a cigarette lighter flared. An unfamiliar face appeared and gave me a start – a swollen face, covered in bruises, like that of a drunkard, was regarding me from one open eye, the other one being hidden by a pouch of purplish blood.

The man was staring at me without hostility, with the semblance of a smile, even.

"They've given me a good going over, haven't they, Pavel?" He picked up a long strip of wood, lit it and stuck it between two planks in the wall. This light, more constant, allowed me to take a better look at him: the deep cut across the base of his nose, the dark crust surrounding his shredded lips and, when he opened his mouth to speak, the fragments of his broken teeth.

"Mark!" I cried out, going up and reaching out to him, as if, by touching him, I could have restored his old face. "But who . . . but how?" I choked on my words for the answer was all too obvious.

Vassin smiled a little more, then grimaced as he spoke; stretching his lips must have been very painful.

"The sergeant made a mistake: he shouldn't have put us together. He'll go and wake Ratinsky, now. And he'll have you locked up in a different shelter. But we've got a few minutes. So, listen to me carefully, Pavel. Luskas and his men torture people to death. I saw Butov after the first interrogation. I didn't recognise him, the way you didn't recognise me just now. He no longer had a face, our commanding officer. Both shoulders broken. His fingers as well. Yesterday he died under torture. His heart. A reservist who brings grub here told me he saw the body . . . Luskas needs to prove that we conspired together to sabotage the mission. It's easy to understand him: if he doesn't

188

get our confessions he'll have to admit his failure. Well, Butov won't say any more now. And from the start I've refused to lie. Luskas knows I'm not all that afraid of dying. So he's going to come down on you like a ton of bricks ..."

I went up to him, seized his hands, shook them. My voice was quaking wildly. "The regimental commander should be informed, Mark! We're not criminals! It's the governor of the camp who's responsible for that girl's escape. It's nothing to do with us!"

Vassin withdrew his hands and I saw that his wrists were bound. Once again, a smile mutated into a grimace of pain.

"Exactly, Pavel. But you know neither the camp governor nor Luskas are ever going to accuse themselves of failing to catch the prisoner. Now ... tell me ... is the fugitive still alive?"

The trapdoor banged open and Ratinsky appeared, followed by two soldiers who blinded us with their electric torches.

"Tie his hands behind his back!" he ordered. I let them do it, certain I would soon go free once I told them the escaped prisoner was dead. I turned back to look at Vassin. He was looking at me, waiting for my reply. "Yes, still," I said quickly in a soft voice. He lowered his head and I saw he was smiling.

As they were transferring me to another shelter I tried to talk to Ratinsky. "Comrade Sub-Lieutenant, I have a very important piece of information to report. Our mission is fulfilled! Could you tell this to Captain Luskas?"

He hissed in hate-filled tones: "You can tell me that tomorrow. The night brings counsel. Especially when you're sleeping in your favourite billet ..." A blow from a rifle butt between my shoulder blades thrust me towards the entrance of a shelter that I recognised in the crosslight of the two torches. Number nineteen.

One of the soldiers went down first, the second pushed me towards the trapdoor and plunged in after me. Ratinsky came down as well, yelling, "Bind his feet and push him over!" The "rag doll" shivered within me. I offered no resistance to the soldiers and, with my ankles bound, I collapsed on the ground. Seeking to adopt the most humble tone of voice possible, I addressed Ratinsky. "Comrade Lieutenant, the escaped prisoner we were pursuing together, I've . . ."

A kick in the face from a boot caused my jaws to snap, eliciting a surprised squeal from me. "But wait!" I still could not believe that the torture was about to begin.

Ratinsky struck me several times, aiming at my head, then my belly. I twisted this way and that, hoping for a respite, so I could tell him the fugitive had been killed . . . It was then that a blow, more violent than the previous ones, struck me below the chin, on that spot where my scar formed a "spider" . . . My vision was clouded. I gulped and for several seconds lay still.

I did not lose consciousness, but, as I emerged from this brief daze, I no longer experienced the alternating pangs of fear and hope that had made me writhe and groan as I was being struck. Dumbfounded, I discovered that the "rag doll" had vanished!

Leaning over me, Ratinsky was yelling abuse with a contorted face, spluttering with rage. I could easily have told him I had killed the fugitive. But I now knew that no torture would have made me do so. Confusedly, I sensed that not lying gave me a chance to believe in that other life whose sense I had guessed at as I watched the woman setting out on her walk towards the ocean.

In a voice made shrill by triumphant hatred Ratinsky informed me: "I was the one who shot down the escaped prisoner! I threw her into the Amgun so as not to have to lug the corpse back here. So don't waste your time telling us any rubbish, you filthy deserter!" He took a step backwards and landed a kick on my head.

I came round at the moment when they were closing the trapdoor again.

With a detachment that surprised me, I felt my body. The buzzing in my ears lasted a moment then stopped. Several blows to my face had surely disfigured me, but I was aware of bleeding in only one place, at the spot where my scar, my "spider", had reopened. The muscles in my stomach and sides had been protected by the "hair shirt" of dried moss I had kept beneath my tunic as protection against the cold. My hands seemed intact, my legs as well.

The situation was easy to assess. Luskas had evidently imposed his version: thanks to him, our team had tracked down the fugitive, but Butov, Vassin and I had tried to scupper the operation. Despite this sabotage, Ratinsky had succeeded in killing the escaped prisoner.

My case was all the more serious since, in addition, I had "deserted"... It had all been carefully stitched up in accordance with the logic of those tribunals that put thousands of "enemies of the people" behind barbed wire every month. All Luskas had to do was to make us confess, or let us die under torture, like Butov, which was doubtless what awaited me, given Ratinsky's fury.

Despite the pain, I experienced joy, almost pride, at not having spoken to him about Elkan. That lie would have dishonoured me, but above all, I now understood, it would have deprived Vassin of that "other life", as he called it. The sunlit bank of a river, the rippling of the autumn leaves and an unending walk, following in the footsteps of a woman whose destination was known only to her.

Shelter number nineteen was familiar to me down to the last nook and cranny. I began my preparations without thinking about the objective or anticipating the dangers. The weeks spent in the taiga had taught me more instinctive survival skills, uncluttered by the timid reasoning that holds back action.

Crawling about in the darkness, I reached the spot beneath the opening for the ventilation shaft that I had broken during my earlier imprisonment. The floor was strewn with fragments from the tube. My wrists were bound, but by scratching about on the ground I managed to pick up a small metal plate. The cutting edge of this, after I had sawn away with it a little, served to free my hands, then my ankles.

I picked up the low bed and propped its timbers against the wall of the shelter, beneath the ventilation opening. Its wooden frame served me as a ladder. I climbed up it, fell, began my ascent again, and managed to cling on to the iron pegs that were the supports for the disintegrated tube. This vertical passage was constricted. The sides of it were studded with hooks, and these enabled me to haul myself up by means of painful spasmodic jerks. I was like a worm working its way through humus. The remnants of the tube ripped my tunic and cut into my skin – I had had to leave my protective layer of dried moss down below.

Halfway up the conduit its diameter seemed to shrink. I could already see the starry sky, I could detect the scent of plants and leaves, but my chest and shoulders would no longer pass through this narrow chimney in the earth. Regardless of the hooks that were tearing me to pieces, I began to screw my body upwards, gaining an inch or two at each rotation . . .

The pain caught up with me when I reached the open air. I lay on the ground, distraught and flayed to ribbons beneath the rags of my clothes. A plaintive voice sounded in my head but, without giving it the chance to assume the shape of a "rag doll", I at once thrust my hands against the ground and stood up, hearing nothing further, apart from the throbbing of the blood in my temples . . .

Shelter number five, which held Vassin, was located not far from the checkpoint. I moved forward, spurred on by the utmost determination, in the hypnotic state that drives us forward when all the limits of danger have been exceeded and are therefore of no account.

As the trapdoor, which was closed with a bar, opened, it emitted a brief creak. I crouched at the top of the staircase and whispered: "Mark, it's me . . . Don't be afraid . . ."

His lighter flared at once, as if he had been expecting me.

I saw he had already managed to free his hands and was currently burning through the cord that held his ankles. He tried to stand up, tottered, and I had to support him. "I was thinking of going to liberate you . . ." he said softly.

In the one-eyed glance he gave me I detected a trace of compassion which enabled me to appreciate the extent to which my face was now a mass of bruises . . . The flame went out. Vassin began again, even more softly. "I was on the point of telling you what a bloody stupid mistake you'd made coming back here. But I see you've already had second thoughts . . . Listen! The checkpoint's very well guarded and, in any case, I wouldn't get far with this smashed knee. So, you must do exactly as I say. Agreed? Then you might have a chance of getting away from here . . ."

In less than a minute we were within sight of the checkpoint. There was a light in the window of this wooden shack. Vassin stopped, felt for my hand in the darkness and shook it. With emotional urgency, he whispered: "On your way, Pavel. I hope you find the girl! If that other life exists . . ."

He limped towards the door and threw it wide open. I heard a shout from the sentry and an oath hurled by the sergeant. Vassin went inside for a moment and the yelling grew louder, followed by the sound of furniture being overturned. The two guards rushed out, attempting to get the better of Vassin, who was fighting ferociously. With one hand he had a grip on the duty guard's rifle and with the other was punching the dumbfounded sergeant in the face. But, above all, he was drawing the two of them towards the thickets, away from the checkpoint.

In the middle of the uproar his voice suddenly rang out: "Go for it!"

I ran up to the shack, went in, stepped across an overturned iron stove, from which burning brands were already setting the floor ablaze, and went out through the opposite door . . .

Plunging into the forest, I could see the light from the blazing checkpoint flickering against the dark wall of the trees. And from far away there came a long cry that no longer sounded like Vassin's voice. A shot rang out. The silence which followed that sudden explosion blended into the calm of the taiga.

AS I RAN, I WAS LIVING THROUGH WHAT A WOUNDED animal might have experienced. Beneath my rags I was almost naked. My back and shoulders were bleeding. My mouth, torn by Ratinsky's blows, flinched with pain when, going down on all fours, I drank water from streams. At night I shook with cold, but I lit only very small fires, so as not to give myself away.

One morning an army helicopter passed above me, skimming the tops of the trees. I did what lynxes and wolves do when danger threatens from above: I lay flat on the ground beneath the broad, low branches of a fir tree. On the evening of the same day the helicopter came back again. Caught on more exposed terrain, I clung to the trunk of an oak tree, blending in with its bark.

For Luskas I was becoming a much more important target than the escaped prisoner. No doubt he was afraid I might reach a town, report his lies to the authorities and dent his irreproachable reputation as a hunter-down of enemies of the people.

The forest was shedding its leaves, giving me less cover for my flight. What saved me was the speed at which I moved and my almost tactile familiarity with the areas I was passing through. And, for the first few days, the fact that I forgot about hunger. Then suddenly I became aware that I lacked food: as I was crossing a tributary of the Amgun, I noticed that the river, quite shallow there, was buckling under my feet, becoming coloured, then turning black. Overcome with giddiness, I stumbled, grasping at the void, my head filled with shouts, chiming bells and, then, suddenly, with long, dull reverberations . . .

The ice-cold water brought me round. I found myself lying on the shore – there were traces in the sand of where I had crawled to get out of the water . . . I stood up, unsteady on my feet, and found enough strength to push several stones together to divert part of the stream. Into the little bay thus formed I dropped crushed shellfish to serve as bait and began lying in wait for my prey, armed with a broken-off branch that ended in a point . . . After several minutes a young taimen appeared. I felt too weak to risk spearing the fish with my stick. I fell upon it, clasping it to my chest in a great fountain of seething water and stirred-up mud. It struggled vigorously and was about to escape my grasp, thanks to its slimy skin. I realised I would never have the chance to catch another. And hence, to eat. And survive. Ducking my head into the water, I bit into its body, between the dorsal fin and the skull.

I got out onto the bank, my hands restraining the writhings of this silvery rocket, my teeth embedded in its vibrating scales . . .

At the end of the day, as I was devouring its flesh, grilled over the embers, I became aware that I had never had thoughts of such sadness and gratitude for a living creature, one that had saved me from dying. In truth, I had never felt myself to be so much at one with the life men refer to as wild, for I myself was now a part of it . . .

From that day on, the world where men hated one another so much, the world of Luskas, of Ratinsky, the world of shelter number nineteen, would begin to fade away, thanks to a distancing process, more mental than physical. One morning, as I resumed my journey, I remembered the way I had been struck in the face and became clearly aware that there was no longer any desire for vengeance within me, no hatred, not even the arrogant temptation to forgive. There was just the sunlit silence of the riverbank as I walked along it, the luminous transparency of the sky and the very faint tinkling of leaves, swathed in frost, slipping away from the branches and coming to rest on the frozen ground with the brief resonance of crystal. Yes, just the ultimate settling-down of silence and light.

This increasing detachment dissipated all anxiety. I knew it would be impossible for me to rediscover Elkan's tracks, let alone locate her shelter. I also knew that the snow was coming, not just a fleeting wintry interlude, but a tide of white with no mild spells, an ice-bound sleep, for nine months. I had no gun, no warm clothes. My only treasure was the lighter Vassin had given me . . . And yet I was not eaten up by anxiety. The whole sense of my flight was now drawing ever closer to that "other life" Vassin had spoken of, the first stage of which was like a walk following in the footsteps of an unknown woman.

AT THE END OF THE FIFTH DAY I REACHED THAT HIGH point where, before turning back, I had watched Elkan going down towards the coast . . . Coming upon the location of our last camp, I decided to spend the night there. A fire, well trodden down and covered with branches, maintained its heat until the morning.

It was still dark when I awoke and, attracted by a breeze that seemed less chilly than the air of the taiga, I went up to the top of the hill. The trees were fewer there, too battered by storms. The stars were reflected on the surface of the water and created the illusion of being scattered along the shoreline and even across the undergrowth. I was beginning to shiver and was on the point of going back to my bed when all of a sudden one of the constellations down below struck me as familiar. Yes, it was a triangle of lights, glowing with more warmth than the icy luminescence of the heavens . . .

I returned to my camp to gather up my belongings. And then I realised that I had no "belongings" to take with me. The goal I was walking towards made them useless.

As I made my way down the hill, the sky began to turn pale,

and took on a mauve tinge. The stars went out and so did the points of light I thought I had glimpsed among the trees.

But I managed to find the spot where I had seen them. The ashes contained no trace of warmth. Elkan must have left the place several days before . . .

Numb as I was with cold, when a voice called out from the forest that sounded much like one heard in a dream, I did not shiver. After several seconds the call came again, more clearly: "Pavel! . . ." I turned round and, seeing nobody, cracked a smile with my bruised mouth: I was dreaming and here, in this wild taiga, some unknown person was hailing me by name!

When she appeared, lowering the barrel of her rifle, I did not move. Subconsciously I was afraid of waking up. But she came forward, undoubtedly reassured to see that it was me, despite my face being covered in dried blood and my rags.

With anxious insistence, she declared, "We must go at once. There won't be another chance like today for a long time . . ."

I straightened up, taken aback. "Go where?" I asked, picturing yet another endless trek through the taiga.

Elkan beckoned me to follow her. We walked down to a channel that flowed into the sea. A long, narrow raft lay on the bank beside it. "It's going to be tough, but we can manage it. Don't ask me any questions. Just try to help me . . ."

We lugged the raft into the water and the current quickly carried us towards the mouth of the channel. The ocean seemed calm – only the effort Elkan had to make to hold the rudder steady betrayed the power of the ebbing tide.

The "rudder", a plank held in suspense between two round

wooden posts, risked becoming disconnected at any moment. I grasped it firmly and this assistance drew a hoarse sigh of relief from Elkan. The sea, slack when we set off, rapidly became animated by a strange swell – waves that were not moving forward, but lifted the raft on their fixed crests and carried it along in fits and starts, following an irregular course. Then the surface became smooth again, creating the impression that we were at a standstill.

Yet the coastline we had just set off from was already far behind us, and our swift, jerky advance was not dependent on eddies that ruffled the surface. A massive, invisible current was carrying us towards a rocky outcrop around which we were trying to steer to the left. "The Southern Island," whispered Elkan. "This is where things will get lively."

As we approached this little island, the very bowels of the sea were ripped open to reveal the entrails of a flood tide, mingling and boiling together to form waves in opposing directions. Our raft was flung this way and that, like a twig in a stream, then suddenly slowed down in an inexplicable respite, avoiding the rocky island and its clouds of seabirds.

In front of us there now loomed up what I had taken for a thick layer of fog – a larger island which rose much higher. "Get a good grip, now!" shouted Elkan, and I saw her words must be taken literally. She seized a rope attached to the raft's timbers. I hastened to grasp another.

The force of the current increased still more. Waves were now breaking over the raft, lashing us, and then rolling back again, as if they had come up against an obstacle in the middle of the empty sea. The wind got up, but it was the fury of the tide that had been carrying us along from the start.

The island was approaching at a petrifying speed, but in front of it a jagged line of half-submerged rocks could be seen, as well as mountains of spray from the backwash. And directly ahead, advancing towards us, there was a wall of rock that looked like the streamlined prow of an ocean liner, poised to cut our already disintegrating raft in two.

We leaned hard against the plank of the rudder to avoid running into it. The raft reared up on a wave, just touched the rock and, glancing off it, was flung onto a shingle beach . . .

The sunlit calm that reigned there seemed improbable, and this was the first and most telling impression made on me by the archipelago of the Shantar Islands. A planet apart, where, within the space of a few yards, as one rounded a cliff, the sea changed, the sky changed, the seasons changed.

Elkan began unloading her luggage onto the shore: rifle, tools, tent canvas . . .

Perplexed by the few belongings we possessed, I asked her, without hiding my bemusement: "So what . . . what are we going to do here?"

Her reply made any further questions trifling.

"We're going to live here."

VI

"WE'RE GOING TO LIVE HERE . . ."

The man broke off at these words, got up, went to fill his teapot, put it back on the fire.

So there I was in the middle of the night, face to face with this Pavel Gartsev, whose tale had revealed, to the adolescent that I was, truths both violent and tender, truths that flew in the face of the world's logic. The logic of a world that had always seemed to me to be closed, monolithic, inescapable.

But now there was this handful of tiny islands, one of them bearing the name of Belichy, "the island of squirrels", with its cliffs, its little mountain, its fast-flowing streams . . . It was home to two people who lived out their lives in opposition to all that human beings longed to possess.

The novelty of such a life was so great that, clumsily, I asked Gartsev: "But on that island . . . what did you . . . do?"

And his voice, echoing those words he had one day heard himself, was imbued with a dreamy simplicity: "What did we do? We lived there . . ."

He must have been aware that the word was well-worn and had lost all its value. He picked up the thread of his story: their early days on that uninhabited archipelago, their first winter, the hardest, because they had barely got settled into the taiga of this island . . . The storms that froze the sea solid from November onwards, erecting a fortress of ice around the island. The fogs that cut them off, at the same time as giving them protection against any assault from the mainland. Immensely powerful ocean currents, waves that broke up ships and sent them to the bottom of the Sea of Okhotsk . . .

I listened to him with all the fascination that any boy of my age would have felt. The shallow sea froze into a solid ice sheet, linking the coast to the archipelago of the Shantar Islands and forming a white desert that animals crossed to come to the island. The brief season without snow that began in June and ended in August. The provisions that had to be gathered in during these few weeks of warmth, if they were to survive the endless months of hibernation. And, when they put out to sea, they risked the deadly threat of a souloi, the name given in that part of the world to a wall of water several yards high that arises where opposing currents meet . . . What also stuck in my memory was the arrival of grey whales close to Belichy Island, in flight from harpoons, seeking shelter in its bays.

I was too young to understand the true significance of their exile. In telling his story, Gartsev slipped in comments, the sense of which eluded me and which would remain mysterious, like a code waiting to be cracked. At the time what he especially wanted to give me an idea of was the utter strangeness of the lives they led on the archipelago.

"Around the Shantar Islands there's a magnetic anomaly.

A compass needle is never still there, it spins round the whole time. This means it can never point north accurately. So how can you expect people on the mainland to understand us?"

On the morning of the third day of our walk together a long upward slope led us to where the forest was less dense. I was now climbing up the track Gartsev had followed so many years before in his pursuit of Elkan . . .

Suddenly the path stopped: we had just reached the summit where it opened out as a promontory. What I saw was beyond words. This dull, misty infinity, where there were no landmarks, contained too much emptiness. The name Mirovia crossed my mind, yes, that legendary prehistoric ocean surrounding the only landmass that then existed, the famous Rodinia that was mentioned in our geography books . . .

Gartsev's voice drew me from my reverie.

"Look there! That's Great Shantar in the middle and Little Shantar off to the left. And facing it, that's Belichy, our island . . ."

I could not really make out the contours of the islands, just hazy outlines hovering above the sea, which might have been taken for a string of clouds. Gartsev took a compass from his pocket and handed it to me. I tried to locate north but the needle kept wandering about, quivering, standing still, then starting to waltz round again, regardless of any magnetic constraint.

I handed the useless instrument back to him and stood there irresolute, as he was too, for it was the moment for us to part, something I found both logical and hard to believe.

Gartsev smiled and there on his neck, quite close to the

carotid artery, I noticed the mark of a scar throbbing gently. His "spider"...

"Right, you'll be going back sticking close to the shore," he said to me, in tones he endeavoured to make casual. "It'll take a little longer, but at least you won't run the risk of getting lost. Whatever you do, don't stray from the coast. And then ... you know, I'm trusting you. I know you won't breathe a word to anyone. So, good luck ..."

He thrust the flat body of a dried fish into my hands, loaded his pack onto his back and strode off. As I did not stir, he turned round and gave me a vaguely military salute. We spent several seconds face to face with one another, trying to find some word or gesture to avoid this being a final parting. At length, Gartsev flung out, in a shout, as if the distance between us were already much greater: "If you come back one day, light three fires here, you know, in a triangle! I'll see them and I'll come and fetch you!"

On my return journey one fragment of his story came back to me: Elkan had waited for him for ten days, reckoning that it would take him five days to reach the training area and five more to return. That is, if he decided to return ... "And what if I'd been several hours late?" he had asked her, much later. She had replied firmly: "I'd have gone to the archipelago without you ... But every evening I'd have lit the fires ..."

AS THE YEARS PASSED, THIS LIFE OF THEIRS ON THE SHANTAR archipelago would take shape in my mind, forming the outline of a world that became more substantial, like a slowly developing photograph.

When I was young, what particularly stayed in my memory was the story of the dangers and ordeals that the two exiles had undergone. The manhunt through the taiga, the rifle shots, the gold prospector's hut where a dead man kept watch. Yes, a tale of adventure, a western. Later I believed I could discern a much more profound and secret truth within it, one that allowed me to guess at the hidden meaning behind those very simple words: "We lived there . . ."

In the spring of 1953, their first spring on the island, when the cold was no longer flaying the lungs at every intake of breath, they thought about the manhunt that would be relaunched against them. Their double escape could not be left unpunished . . . They set up hiding places, built a boat, so that, if danger threatened, they could take refuge on Little Shantar Island, which was more densely forested.

In June the sea began to break free of ice. In July navigation became possible and every day they expected to see motor boats appearing in the Lindholm Strait, heading towards Belichy . . . They lit fires only under cover and took it in turns to mount guard – the same as during the pursuit led by Luskas, as they would remark.

Summer was beginning to fade, the snows would soon return, but there was no sign of any kind of attack in preparation. No hedge-hopping overflights by helicopters, no craft approaching by sea.

"It's as if the nuclear war has already taken place," thought Gartsev. "And no-one's survived . . . Or else, as if there's been a great change in the country."

He was not altogether wrong.

At the end of August they risked an expedition, landed on the mainland and travelled on foot as far as the village of Tugur. Gartsev remained in the taiga (a man is always more conspicuous, they thought). Elkan went on reconnaissance and had the luck to encounter one of her own people, an elderly Nigidale woman from a clan that lived on the banks of the Amgun. They spoke to one another in their native language and it was in this Tungus dialect, common to just a few hundred people, that the staggering news was broken, an event already common knowledge throughout the world: Stalin was dead!

His demise, in March, had caused a shockwave, setting off a chain of consequences that would take years to unfold. But already, from the first days of summer, the gates of the camps had been partly thrown open. A flood of prisoners had surged out, eager to get away from Siberia. For the most part it was criminal offenders who had been released. Drunk with freedom, often after twenty years of penal servitude, they gave no quarter. Pillage, rape, murder – the towns barricaded themselves in, the army fired into the crowds and machine guns mowed down hordes of them, as they broke through roadblocks and flung themselves, bare-handed, against bayonets, in an onward surge, by day and by night, towards the lights of places of habitation . . .

So this was not the moment, thought Elkan, for the authorities to be concerned about two fugitives on their wild island.

She broke the news to Gartsev. While he had been waiting, he had noticed a lorry packed with soldiers driving past on the road to Tugur . . . They decided to make their way back via pathways through the forest. When they halted beside a ford they came upon a scene of carnage: a number of men and women lay there, freed prisoners, who had doubtless been fired on by machine guns from a helicopter. There were no cartridge cases lying on the ground.

This was how Elkan and Gartsev obtained identity documents, with photographs that more or less resembled them.

They had hardly left the spot when they heard the sound of a helicopter's blades, and the shadow of an aircraft passed over the trees, as if the pilot had wanted to check on the results of the execution.

On their way back towards the ocean, they needed no words to understand one another and maintained a rapid pace, wanting to waste no time. I remember that Gartsev used precisely this expression when he was telling his story: "We wanted to waste no time," and I believed he was talking about practical constraints – a military roadblock to avoid, the tide holding them back from setting sail . . .

It took me many years of allowing my memories to settle for me to discern, in this banal phrase, the choice to which their whole lives were committed, one whose radical force I found troubling: they wanted to waste no time in the world they had left behind!

No, Gartsev had never complained about the cruelty of the regime, nor the military absurdities of History, he who had once made a study of "the legitimacy of revolutionary violence". But as he walked along at Elkan's side, he was reflecting on the whole vast game that included a helicopter hovering above murdered prisoners; as well as shelter number nineteen, where he had almost suffocated to death while they were simulating atomic warfare; and the two actual bombs that had exposed millions of innocent people in Japan to radiation; and Captain Luskas, who used to shoot condemned men in the back of the neck and then cried out in his sleep; and that "rag doll" lurking within every one of us, stirring up our fears, our desires, our selfishness . . .

"And this woman, Elkan," Gartsev said to himself, "whom I sought to kill, so as to earn a role in the farcical charade of a world in which men have lived in mutual hatred since the beginning of time."

Their exile was less about a fear of being arrested and thrown into a camp than it was about a refusal to take part in any such games.

WHEN I WAS YOUNG MY THOUGHTS OFTEN STRAYED BACK to those hermits on the Shantar Islands. At one time their exile seemed to me incomprehensible, even terrifying. To cut yourself off from society, to hide away amid ice and snow on a tiny island surrounded by a raging ocean! To turn your back on the exciting spectacle of life, its dramas, its rivalries. I was then at an age when the multiple possibilities of life are dazzling and the variety of poses one can adopt is intoxicating. When changing roles gives the impression of freedom. When dividing one's persona between a thousand different relationships is perceived as an enrichment of life.

I felt I was enjoying all that Gartsev and Elkan would never know.

Then all at once, with no consideration for my own self-esteem, the tables were turned: every day that passed was taking me further and further away from the chance to enjoy and understand the things they had enjoyed and understood.

This was nothing to do with the number of "experiences" they had, a value so prized by modern life. Nor about some vague wisdom derived from one such exotic experience. Their daily life was rough and simple, not directed towards any edifying goal. They needed to find good mica for the windows of their house, and when the severest frosts came, install "double glazing", cut from slabs of ice. When they lacked cartridges, they shot game with bows and arrows and Gartsev came to prefer this soundless way of hunting. At low tide fish trapped among the rocks were easy to catch and in the autumn the forest teemed with berries. Elkan baked what they used as bread: types of dough made from grasses, dried mushrooms, pine shoots.

I remember how, in talking about this life, Gartsev confided to me with an amazed smile, "I would never have thought man needed so little."

With the fading away of the Stalin era the situation changed. Gartsev now visited the mainland at Tugur, where people took him for a game warden. He even went as far as Nikolayevsk. Yet after each of those rare trips, he would return to the Shantar Islands "like a sleepwalker waking up", as he said. And such news as reached them from the outside world indicated that mankind was remaining true to its old ways: since the Korean War, enough bombs had been built to burn the planet to a cinder a hundred times over and meanwhile villages and their inhabitants were being incinerated with napalm, forests were being transformed into deserts and oceans into sewage works. Newspapers purchased in Nikolayevsk spoke of the Vietnam War; of pollution; of atomic weapons tests; of how a cellulose combine that was poisoning Lake Baikal had exceeded its five-year plan; of the fact that the Earth's population would soon reach four billion ...

These threats to the planet did not preclude the odd threat of a much more modest variety, so humanly banal as to be almost excusable. Like a certain man at the wheel of an off-road vehicle. Gartsev encountered him one morning, as he was leaving Tugur. "You there," shouted this petty despot. "I work in the Forestry Management and I know all the game wardens. But I've never seen you before!" And he stared at him with the arrogance of a hostile inquisitor.

On the road home Gartsev thought about Luskas and Ratinsky ... The same human nature, compounded of suspicion, aggressiveness and treachery. "Stalin's dead. Almost twenty years have passed. And yet this fir tree manager is still busy unmasking enemies of the people ..."

That day, on account of the timing of the tide, it was already dusk when Gartsev left the mainland. His vessel with its square sail rode smoothly over the swell, slipped along in the lee of the little Southern Island, and sped towards Belichy. Through the mist that hung over the archipelago, he could make out the three shining dots. A triangle of fires. "The constellation of our very own sky," he thought, with a tenderness for which the world he had just left behind had no word.

WHAT FASCINATED ME MOST ABOUT THEIR EXILE WAS THE reckless defiance with which they had challenged fate. The glorious madness of their flight . . .

It took me long years to grasp that it was the life we were all living that was mad! Warped by ingrained hatred and violence that had become a lifestyle, mired in the white lies and obscene truths of wars. I remember mentioning this in conversation one day with an American friend, a convinced pacifist. She countered my remarks by speaking of the need for "humanitarian bombing" . . . I forget whether we were talking about Belgrade or Baghdad at the time. Curiously enough, this reminded me of the subject of the thesis Pavel Gartsev had been writing all those years before, yes, "the legitimacy of revolutionary violence" . . .

It was not the two fugitives but mankind itself that was going off the rails, in a flight that was suicidal.

As I grew older, with the inevitable acceptance of the rules of the game, this vivid insight of mine faded. The occasional flashes of memory that still came back to me from the story Gartsev had told me that night now mutated into regrets, reproaches. Yes, another life was possible, Elkan and Gartsev had shown this with the humble means at their disposal as outlaws, but no-one would ever know about it and the world would continue to drift, distancing itself ever further from the Shantar archipelago.

I went back to far eastern Siberia in August 2003, forty years after my encounter with Pavel Gartsev. A Russian magazine had announced the building of a tidal power station in the Gulf of Tugur . . . So it was the last chance to revisit the past while it was still more or less intact.

I had little hope of finding the exiles of the Shantar Islands alive. The harshness of the climate and their privations would not have favoured a particularly long life.

When I reached Tugur I could see that the village had been spared the political upheavals of recent years. Here it amounted to no more than changes to the signs: the adjective "Soviet" being replaced by "Russian" . . .

The edge tool workshop, my former lodging house, even seemed to have been brightened up and now, repainted, was functioning as a garage for four-by-fours. And, notably, there was, as yet, no devastation on view from any construction site.

A pale sun, the infinite expanse of the sea and, behind it, the taiga, endlessly waiting there. Time abolished.

Sasha, who is twenty-seven and in whose home I am renting a room, lives with his wife and their two sons in a large izba, a little outside the village. His wife, a Nivkh woman, from one

217

of the local peoples, must look like Elkan, I tell myself: a beautiful face with fine features, slanted eyes and cheekbones tanned by the sun and wind. Her husband is clearly of mixed race. Unusually for natives of the area, he is tall, with the narrow dark eyes of a Mongol but, in contrast, fair, reddish hair.

Aware that I am eyeing him closely, he explains this, both embarrassed to be talking about his physical appearance and proud to be initiating me into the secrets of the country.

"There are some people here who have Scandinavian blood. Like me . . ."

"Scandinavian?"

Calling to mind the seven thousand miles that lie between Sweden and the Pacific coast, I study my host's features: this Siberian, a descendant of the Vikings?

He smiles, happy to amaze me.

"You know of Lindholm? Otto Lindholm, the navigator. He was a Finn who explored our coastline and finally settled in Vladivostok. His sailors did the same and married women from our country. Before the Revolution Lindholm was famous. He gave great assistance to the Russian fleet and Tsar Nicolas II regarded him as his friend . . . The strait between the mainland and the Shantar Islands bears his name, of course . . .

Sasha continues to give me interesting details of local history, but all I can think about now is asking him the vital question: could he take me to Belichy Island? And does he know if Gartsev and Elkan are still there?

Because he has just mentioned the archipelago in passing, I cut in, rather hastily.

"But . . . is it possible to cross it, that strait? And go to . . . I don't know . . . to Belichy Island, for example?"

Forty years on, I sense within myself a fear of betraying the exiles' secret.

Sasha looks away and speaks to his sons, who are unravelling the tangled rope around an anchor on the floor.

"Off you go, lads. You can finish that tomorrow. It's time for bed now."

His wife gets up, hustles the children towards the door and leaves the room. So our subject merits a discussion man to man.

"Great Shantar Island is more than sixty miles from here by sea. That's quite some way . . . As soon as you move out of the Gulf of Tugur the currents pull you along worse than a tugboat. Little Shantar is closer, but, between that island and Belichy, there's a very dangerous stretch where you take your life in your hands. And then there are rocks. There are a lot of them just below the surface. In the time it takes to strike a match and light up – that's it – you find you have a hole in your side! And if that happens you can forget any idea of getting back to the mainland. There's no mobile network. The bears will come before any help does . . ."

To leave Tugur without having seen the Shantar Islands seems to me unthinkable. In refusing to go, perhaps Sasha is just holding out for some remuneration. I hesitate, afraid of offending him.

"Listen . . . I realise that fuel must be hard to come by in these parts . . . I'll pay what's needed. And if one needs baksheesh for the local mayor that could be arranged . . ."

He sits up straight in his chair – his face has grown more sombre. I have just been guilty of a category confusion: what governs any decision about a voyage to the Shantars will be remote from material considerations.

His voice grows distant and for a moment I believe he is going to cut our discussion short and wish me goodnight.

"The archipelago is not a destination like any other . . . The tides have to be carefully taken account of and so does the north-west wind. That's the worst, it's the one that blows down from the mountains of Yakutia . . ."

I hold back from speaking, so as not to force his hand.

"But why, in fact . . . Why do you want to go to the Shantar Islands?" he asks, with a strange element of constraint in his voice.

Should I tell him I'm an ethnologist fascinated by the native peoples of eastern Siberia and the Nigidales in particular? That lie, I'm sure, would doom my project. All the more because the whole meaning of Gartsev and Elkan's life in exile was nothing to do with the folklore exoticism of shamans and such-like festivals of the Bear . . . I decide to tell him the truth.

"The fact is . . . I knew two people who lived on Belichy Island . . ."

Sasha's words echo mine. "So did I. I knew them, too . . ."

Realising that I myself had never set eyes on Elkan, I start again, talking about my encounter with Gartsev in the taiga, and our conversation that night . . .

I note that, for a young man, these events from long ago have the status of a legend. And also a guarantee of confidence, a confession, as between initiates.

Spurred on by the sharing of these memories, we head out towards the sea, as if the past might find living embodiment in that August evening. Over to the west the light picks out the dark shadow of the mountains, the purple crenellations of the taiga. Sasha seems to be feeling for his words and I realise that he has never before had the opportunity to tell this story.

"When the U.S.S.R. exploded I was fourteen and living with my parents in Nikolayevsk. Things fell apart more violently there than in Moscow. All enterprises closed down. People survived by petty dealing, everyone in his own corner. In despair, people drank and committed suicide. My parents stuck it out for a time, then they caved in like the others: drink, little schemes for buying yourself one more bottle. One morning they were found at a bus stop, dead from the cold. I was already living on the street in a gang that was re-selling drugs. I'd got hooked on dope and I'd never have been able to kick the habit if, one day . . . In fact, it was in a shop, I noticed a guy who looked like either a sable hunter or a gold prospector. I nicked his bag and ran off and I couldn't figure out how, suddenly, he wasn't behind me but there in front of me. It's an old trapper's trick. He grabbed my collar and said to me, very calmly: 'Either you come with me or I'll kill you.' I hadn't much choice really and, in any case, sleeping out in the taiga or in a damp cellar, as I'd been doing for weeks, made no great difference . . . We went to Tugur by helicopter, then three days' walk through the forest and finally we crossed by boat to Belichy . . . I spent nine months there. Every evening Gartsev gave me lessons in all the subjects I'd bunked off from at school. Elkan helped me to get to know the taiga, which I'd always been wary of, like all townies. At the end of the following summer Gartsev took me to Nikolayevsk and got me into a boarding school where, thanks to all his teaching, I was able to go straight into a more senior class. Later on, at university in Khabarovsk, I got the feeling that I had nothing more to learn beyond what the archipelago had already taught me. I dropped out and came and settled here in Tugur. They were looking for a game warden at the time. Once or twice every summer I'd go over to the Shantar Islands. Sometimes Gartsev and Elkan would come and spend a night with us, if bad weather was keeping them on the mainland. But I sensed that their real life was over there ..."

He falls silent. No sound can be heard now beyond the hiss of the waves obliquely smoothing the sand, and the stray cries uttered by birds as they flit from the last of the light over the ocean to the taiga, steeped in darkness. I am naturally eager to know if the couple are still living on the Shantar Islands, but his silence is too heavy with words as yet unspoken. I prefer to go back to the past.

"They had to fight to survive in those conditions, didn't they?"

With an unexpected smile Sasha resumes his story: "On Belichy there's a hill over twelve hundred feet high. Gartsev had set up a propeller there, linked to a dynamo and, as there's never any shortage of wind on the islands, they had access to a little electricity, enough to light up a couple of bulbs. It was thanks to that windmill that I could read in the evenings ..."

He begins speaking more rapidly – as if he were in a hurry

to call to mind all the details before they faded. The stout ropes that Elkan made from long strands of seaweed, plaited and dried . . . Their wooden house "with a double shell", as Gartsev used to say, for, instead of abandoning their original shelter, they had constructed covered passages all around it, thus encasing it within a larger house, which made this interlocking dwelling invulnerable to the fiercest blizzards . . . Then there was the young seal they had rescued from under the noses of wolves . . . And the grey whales that came to "blow" a few yards from their bay. Perched on a rock, Elkan would imitate their breathing and on summer nights she even used to stroke the backs of whale calves as they slept . . .

Sasha relates all this in a jumble of facts, either real or only dreamed of, giving the impression that his storyteller's brio is a way of putting off the need to tell me what eventually happened to the exiles.

Suddenly his flow of words stumbles, as if encountering an obstacle: how can he convey the mystery of their lives?

Vexed, he strides along the foreshore, looking as if he has an urge to get closer to the archipelago that lies hidden beyond where the shoreline curves round.

"The plain truth of the matter is simple. Having survived persecution under Stalin, they could never have imagined that something worse might happen now, in our liberal era. Two years ago, a Sino-Russian company had the idea of setting up cruises around the Sea of Okhotsk, along the lines of: 'Have fun while feasting your eyes on the volcanoes of Kamchatka and the town of Magadan, former capital of the Gulag.' A visit to the Shantar Islands was included in the itinerary. The organisers had no use for two old people hanging on to their island. They tried to dislodge them by offering them a lump sum. But the response was clear: no crowds of tourists on this fragile terrain. A week later a gang of thugs came and there was a gunfight. I was in Nikolayevsk at the time. On my return I jumped into my boat and headed for the archipelago . . ."

He takes a deep breath, clears his throat and speaks in broken tones.

"Their house had been burned, their three dogs shot. And I never found Gartsev's vessel. Nor their bodies. Thrown into the sea or else buried in the taiga? I've no idea . . . But . . ."

He coughs, and again chokes back a sob.

"But I knew that, despite their age, Gartsev and Elkan were not ones to let people get the better of them. I've been told that the bastards who'd attacked them later turned up at the hospital in Tugur to be treated for arrow wounds. No, that couple wouldn't have let themselves be killed without putting up a fight . . . And then Gartsev had another boat, hidden in a bay a mile or two from their house. I went there . . ."

His voice shakes, as it rises to an excited shout.

"The boat was no longer there! Yes, I'm sure they managed to get away . . . So where could they go? Well, there were a lot of possibilities. First of all, somewhere else in the archipelago. There are at least fifteen islands. Mind you, in that case, they'd have shown themselves long ago. They'd have come to my house in Tugur. So it's more likely that they left the islands and sailed along the coast, heading west at first, then going up towards the north. There are some completely wild places up there. Or else, with the south wind, they might possibly have reached St Jonas' Island . . ."

He breaks off, sits down on a tree trunk washed up onto the shore, his head bowed, doubtless aware of the improbability of all these various routes to safety. St Jonas' Island . . . A cluster of rocks in the middle of that icy sea – even a powerful and well-equipped vessel would take weeks to locate it. A needle in a haystack.

Sasha knows this, but he wants to hold on to some hope at all costs. It is more than the simple wish not to abandon the two exiles to death and oblivion. It is, rather, a dream that helps him to live: the pale light of dawn, a square sail, two figures silhouetted in a boat, slowly approaching a coastline.

Night has fallen. High above the mountains a cluster of stars appears to be trembling, it makes me think of the fires arranged in a triangle, as a signal . . .

Sasha gets up, turns his head first to the right, then to the left, then gazes up at the sky. His voice is uncertain, as if he were afraid of not being able to keep his promise.

"We could go tomorrow. Very early in the morning. About 3.30 a.m. At least you'll see Belichy. Their island . . ."

I REMAIN WIDE AWAKE, AS INCREASINGLY VIVID FLASHES of memory cross my mind. A fisherman rescued by Gartsev and Elkan. They look after him and take him back to the mainland, wondering whether he will report their presence on the archipelago to the authorities. The shipwreck victim keeps their secret and they do not know whether this is because the era when denouncing suspects was obligatory has passed, or, quite simply, thanks to one man's decency . . . Three years later, during a particularly harsh winter, he comes to visit them, making the sixty-mile crossing on skis: "I wanted to see if you needed anything . . ."

One day their roof is torn off in a violent snowstorm: they take refuge in their "inner house", the old heart of their dwelling . . .

And it is in that refuge that they talk about the past. Not so as to revive old grievances against those who persecuted them, but simply in order to marvel at the thousand coincidences that life throws up. In 1952, in the middle of the Korean War, the veteran reservist Gartsev ends up at a military location where the soldiers are being trained to survive an atomic attack. On account of this military exercise, the local Nigidale population have been displaced, expelled from their lands . . . The people are resigned, agree to join a kolkhoz. But one young woman, Elkan, refuses, rebels. She is sent to a camp. As she is being transferred, she escapes, and, during the night, when crossing the territory of the training area, she hears shouts "coming from under my feet", she would later tell Gartsev. She would see a hole in the ground and, without knowing that this was a ventilation shaft, remove the clods of earth blocking it. Shelter number nineteen . . .

They recall this and smile. The storm shakes the door and rattles the mica windowpanes with volleys of snow. The dogs are asleep by the fire. Their infusion of herbs and pine shoots is steeping in the pot. When the wind dies down the stillness of the night is broken by loud cracking sounds – as tree trunks split open under pressure from the frozen sap. "So it must be minus at least 45, if not minus 50°C . . ." Gartsev thinks. In the darkness he clasps Elkan's hand. She is asleep, her long black hair shines, caught in a beam of moonlight. "We're going to live here," he remembers. And he realises that it is only here, on the Shantar Islands, that he has grasped the true meaning of the word . . .

And then there is that rocky outcrop on one of their island's headlands. In the spring, when the wind blows from the northwest, the ocean hurls itself against this side of the cape and the foam from the waves freezes in the air and lacerates the face of anyone who dares to sail into this icy inferno. As you round the headland, you move into a bay sheltered by high cliffs. Sunlight, calm, a smooth sea, it is almost hot there, as if it were summer. Elkan often comes here to wait for Gartsev, on his return from the mainland . . . This place seems to be oblivious of squalls, but also of the world's cruelty. And of time.

Suddenly, as if reality were breaking in, Sasha's words come back to me: they were killed, the hermits of the Shantar Islands. That is, unless – a faint hope – they were able to escape in a dinghy, twelve feet long, braving a sea where every year dozens of boats go down. But even if this final escape had been successful, what irony! They would be fleeing by going back to the lands where, in the old days, the watchtowers of the camps once stood tall . . .

Sasha wakes me at about 3 a.m. The darkness outside the windows is dense, coal-black, as if during the night the taiga had surrounded the house. Drinking very strong, very sweet tea, I conceive of our voyage through this night in mourning as an elegiac ceremony of leave-taking.

At the start of our journey this notion stays with me. The boat moves along with the monotonous drone of its two outboard motors. Sasha is silent, his eyes fixed on the sombre line of the coast, which rears up to the right of us, bleak and unmoving. I try to penetrate the gloom, to make out the landmarks by which we steer, but the darkness of the shoreline obscures the frontier between the sea, the beach and, further off, the forest and the mountains. Before we left, I had looked at the map: our village is located at the head of a gulf, a huge fjord, in fact, which we have to emerge from, following its coastline for some thirty miles. Gartsev and Elkan, for their part, travelled the length of it on foot through the forest until they reached the headland where it juts out further into the sea, forming a promontory. After three days' walk through the taiga, all they had to do was to cross the Lindholm Strait, a distance of little more than three miles.

"Get some sleep," Sasha advises me. "We've got a good couple of hours before it starts to get light at all. Once we emerge from the gulf we'll get no more rest."

I lie down on a narrow bench across from his seat as steersman. The cabin is narrow, with a very low ceiling, and I can see nothing that looks like a radio . . . Sleep overtakes me like a soothing caress given to a child: no longer worrying about anything, no longer thinking about the dangers, blending with the reassuring vibration of the motors. I know that we are travelling at about twenty miles an hour, I try to calculate how long the journey will take, I get confused, fall asleep.

I feel a sudden jolt right through my body and the boat changes course, swinging round in a circle to absorb the impact of the wave that follows. I sit up, and press my forehead against the cabin window. Beyond the fountains of spray an ashen luminescence can be perceived, but it is quite impossible to make out shapes, colours, distances. The sky and the ocean are joined together in the same pewter greyness. A strand of seaweed, stuck to the window, stirs, flutters and finally flies away, carried off by a squall of wind . . .

"We've just left the Gulf of Tugur," Sasha calls out to me,

above the noise of the motors. "It's going to get rough now!"

As if in response to his words, a wave hits us head-on, the boat plunges, a torrent washes over the open deck behind the cabin, causing water to flood in under the cabin door. "We need to bail!" Sasha kicks a plastic bucket towards me. I open one of the halves of the door and instinctively retreat, feeling with my free hand for something to hold on to.

Seen from inside, everything was blended together in the same pale fluid light. Outside, this unity flies apart – the sea swells, explodes, crumples up into crests of foam, billows into a swift ripening of masses of water that show their greenish entrails, lashing me with salt, drawing the boat into a sideways slide that causes it to collide with a retreating wave. High above all this turbulence, the sky remains serenely impassive with its even tonality of steel, a dull mirror reflecting the image of a speck of dust – our boat – lost in the middle of nothingness. The sun has not yet risen and this light, devoid of all nuance, is that of an unknown planet wholly covered by an ocean from primordial times ...

I am managing to fling out the water, as it continues to flood in aft of the cabin. The wind, laden with humidity, blinds me, I skid, I stoop, bailing out the flow of water that sweeps across the boat from one side to the other. A wave, higher than the rest, lifts up the stern – the propellers from the outboard motors, hoisted up into the air, spin furiously with a frenzied grinding sound. I crouch down so as not to topple over and it is at this moment that Sasha opens the door and yells: "Come in quickly! It's the souloi!"

Inside the cabin, as we suddenly slow down, I stumble and collapse onto the bench. Outside the door, one of the wings of which has got stuck, I see a wall of water rising up on the port side, very close to the boat. A wave twelve feet high that seems unmoving, like a screen, along which we are slipping, battling against a current not betrayed by any swell. The wall is almost transparent and its jade thickness is lit up by the sunrise – I even have time to glimpse the silvery glint of a fish . . .

Sasha turns the wheel abruptly to the right, the boat lists, a powerful cascade spills towards the stern. We are no longer moving forwards, but revolving on the spot, on a boiling sea. "Souloi . . ." Sasha shouts again and I detect less alarm in his tone of voice than before. He is steering standing up now, with his head thrust through the broad hatch that he has opened in the roof. His long, russet, "Scandinavian" locks are flapping in the salty air like a sail starved of wind.

The storm begins to die down. I wriggle my way outside again and do not recognise the sea. A distinct frontier divides it in two: far away in the distance it is turbulent and dark, here, where we are crossing, it is as calm as a millpond. I turn to look ahead. I have lost my bearings now and, incredulous, I try to take it all in with one stunned gaze.

A tawny, jasperoid cliff looms above us, like a great ship. The mass of it is streaked with the white of seabirds' wings. The island lies ahead of us, clearly visible, with its forest, its mountain and its necklace of reefs just above the surface, around which Sasha contrives to steer us, reducing speed still further.

We land in a bay, draw the boat up into a space between two rocks, and take our first staggering steps along the shore of Belichy Island.

"Here ... This is their country ..."

Sasha says it softly, as if afraid the words might distort what we are seeing.

I should like to run along the beach, walk all round the island, beat a path through the forest, yes, get to know everything, observe everything! Sasha senses my impatience, his face grows tense, and, looking northwards, he points towards a heavily laden, murky horizon.

"With a wind like today's, we're in for a soaking in an hour's time ..."

He leaves me at the foot of the rocks, goes back to the boat. The blades of one of the propellers have been damaged by catching on a reef – the propellor needs to be changed.

The wind can barely be felt beneath the cliff where the rock is already warmed by the sun. Leaning against its battered surface, I no longer have any desire to explore the place. I sense that the intimate life of the two exiles must remain inviolate at all costs. Above all, after their death. Or their departure? I think of the torched house, the remnants of a life that will soon be offered up to the snap-happy curiosity of cruise passengers.

Elkan and Gartsev . . . What will truly remain of their presence under this sky, on this island some seven miles long, set in an ocean that is sometimes raging with storms, sometimes frozen over with ice? Sasha has told me about the charred timbers of their refuge, their vanished boats, the dispersal of the things that helped them to survive . . .

So, nothing of that? Nothing. No trace!

I try to picture their love, their affection. But such a sentimental reconstruction, I know, will never express the essence of the attachment there was between them. At best it could only soften the pain, my own, that of Sasha.

I close my eyes beneath the glowing light reflected off the water. The sea gently stirs the tiny pebbles on the beach . . . Elkan used to wait here for the square sail to appear. When he had got to the furthest extremity of the mainland, Gartsev would light three fires and, if the sea was too rough, for several days this triangle would be the signal for his imminent return. The sun would reappear, the ocean would grow calm and Elkan would come to this bay in the shelter of the cliff. She kept her eyes fixed on the outline of the sail in the misty air and when the craft landed they both understood that this moment, lit by a crimson, jasper glow, was the very essence of their life. Of this other life.

The rain begins to fall, ahead of Sasha's forecast. A heavy, monotonous rain, whose silvery curtain calms the wind, weakens the swell.

We leave without delay, afraid of being caught by the night. Sasha remains standing, his head thrust through the hatch in the cabin roof, his hands almost unmoving on the wheel. In this fixed position he really resembles one of his Viking ancestors, at large on these far eastern seas, more remote for them than Greenland or America . . . I settle in the stern to watch the islands slowly fading behind the sombre downpour of the rain.

And I do not realise that, instead of heading into the Gulf of Tugur, Sasha is deviating to the left towards the tip of the peninsula.

We go down onto the shore and, without any need to confer, we gather up branches and light three fires, facing the island of Belichy.

THE ONLY LETTER THAT EVER REACHED ME FROM TUGUR can be summarised in a few sentences. Sasha wrote that a fisherman, sailing round the archipelago, just before the coming of the ice, had noticed a square sail travelling along the northern shore of the Lindholm Strait...

Reading his account of this, so vibrant with hope and so barely realistic, I told myself that the sight of this sailing ship, amid the luminous mists of the Shantar Islands, was doubtless the most beautiful trace that a love between two people could leave among the living.

ANDREÏ MAKINE was born in Siberia, but writes in French. *Le Testament Français* was the winner of the Prix Goncourt and the Prix Médicis, and was the first novel to win both of these prestigious awards. His novels have been translated into more than forty languages. His novel *A Life's Music* won the Grand Prix RTL-Live and the novels *The Woman Who Waited* and *Brief Loves that Live Forever* were shortlisted for the Dublin IMPAC Literary Award in 2008 and 2015.

GEOFFREY STRACHAN has translated all of Andreï Makine's novels published in English to date. He was awarded the Scott Moncrieff Prize for his translation of *Le Testament Français*. His translations also include novels by Jérôme Ferrari, Nathacha Appanah and Yasmina Reza.

A New Library from MacLehose Press

This book is part of a new international library for literature in translation. MacLehose Press has become known for its wide-ranging list of best-selling European crime writers, eclectic non-fiction and winners of the Nobel and Independent Foreign Fiction prizes, and for the many awards given to our translators. In their own countries, our writers are celebrated as the very best.

Join us on our journey to **READ THE WORLD**.

www.maclehosepress.com